Lee knew he had to face reality.

"I know it's too late and I know that words are easy, but I want to tell you that I'm so sorry for what I did to your father," he said. "I wish…I wish I could turn back time. Do it over again."

Abby glanced at him. "You're not the only one who wishes that."

The bitterness in her voice made him wait a beat to give the moment some weight.

"My father spent a lot of time struggling with pain," she continued. "He was a broken man after that. My parents' marriage couldn't hold together. What you did to my family…me and my brother—" She stopped there, holding up her hand as if trying to stop the memories.

Lee knew he deserved every bit of her derision, but he would be lying if he said he wasn't hurt by it.

At one time Abby had been important to him. Her poor opinion of him hurt almost as much as the loss of his fre

"I better go," she sa

But he wished she'

Carolyne Aarsen and her husband, Richard, live on a small ranch in northern Alberta, where they have raised four children and numerous foster children and are still raising cattle. Carolyne crafts her stories in an office with a large west-facing window, through which she can watch the changing seasons while struggling to make her words obey.

Books by Carolyne Aarsen

Love Inspired

Refuge Ranch

Hearts of Hartley Creek

Home to Hartley Creek

Visit the Author Profile page at Harlequin.com for more titles.

The Cowboy's Homecoming

Carolyne Aarsen

Recycling programs for this product may not exist in your area.

LOVE INSPIRED BOOKS

ISBN-13: 978-0-373-81840-2

The Cowboy's Homecoming

Copyright © 2015 by Carolyne Aarsen

www.Harlequin.com

Printed in U.S.A.

Bear with each other and forgive one another
if any of you has a grievance against someone.
Forgive as the Lord forgave you.
—*Colossians* 3:13

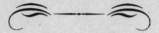

For all those who struggle with hurts
and forgiveness.

Chapter One

All he needed was a few more minutes. A slice of time to make the shift from Lee Bannister, ex-con, to Lee Bannister—wayward son coming home.

And he knew exactly where to get it.

Lee feathered the brakes of his pickup as his eyes scanned the ditch to his right. It had been years since he was in this part of Montana, but when he rounded another curve, he saw the grass-covered approach he'd been looking for. Coming to a full stop, he could just make out the twin tracks of a road heading through a break in the trees. He parked his truck, two wheels well into the ditch so that any motorist cresting the hill could easily pass it.

Once he stepped out, he took a moment to appreciate the warm summer sun beating down on his head, the melody of the blackbirds twittering in the aspen trees.

The air held the tang of pine and warm grass and he let it seep through him as he walked the overgrown trail. Every muffled fall of his boots on the grass eased away the clang and clamor of rig work that surrounded him every waking hour.

He ducked, brushing aside a branch that almost slapped him in the face, looking forward to the solitude and the view at the end of the trail. Few people knew about the lookout point he was headed to. Only his sisters and his parents and a couple of the guys Lee had partied with in high school.

Lee pushed the thought back. Though he knew other bits of history would crowd in on his consciousness during this trip back to the ranch, he intended not to jog too many memories of the past while he was here. He had come to help his sister celebrate her wedding and his parents commemorate the one hundred and fiftieth anniversary of the ranch. And that was it. He had no desire to reminisce about the good old days with any of his friends.

He stepped over a fallen tree and skirted another tangle of small brush. A few more steps and he stopped, breathing deeply.

It was as if the world had fallen away below his feet.

Granite mountains, solid and stately, their jagged peaks still etched with winter snow, cradled the basin below him, simultaneously creating a majesty and a sense of security.

The Saddle River unspooled below him, a winding ribbon of silver meandering through the valley as poplar and spruce trees crowded its banks. To his left lay the town of Saddlebank, its streets dotted with trees and paralleling the railroad that followed the river. From here he could make out Main Street with its brick buildings and, in the dead center of town, Mercy Park with its requisite memorial and gazebo. Past the park and above the trees, he could see the steeple of Saddle Community Church to one side, the cross and bell of the Catholic church on the other. Beyond Saddlebank and to his right, the rest of the valley was taken up with ranches—one of which, Refuge Ranch, was his final destination.

But not yet.

Lee drew another long, slow breath, letting the utter peace and splendor of the view feed his wounded and weary soul.

"Then sings my soul," he whispered, lowering himself to a large rock worn smooth by the winds that could bluster through the valley.

The words of an old hymn that his father would sing when they were outside, working on the ranch, returned. He let his mind sift back, let the recollections he struggled so hard to keep at bay wash over him.

In prison, the memories had hurt too much. The contrast between the confines of a drab cell and the mind-numbing routine, to this space and emptiness and peace hurt too much, so he kept the disparate parts of his life compartmentalized in order to survive.

Now he'd been out for five years and he still never took for granted the ability to go to bed when he wanted. Get up when he wanted. Eat what he wanted and do what he wanted when work was over.

Lee sighed. He knew coming back here would be bittersweet. It would be both a reminder of what he'd lost because of his irresponsibility, but also a reminder of what had always been available to him. Family, community and the unconditional love of his parents and, most important, his sustaining relationship with God.

He let his eyes drift over a view that he had, for so many years, considered home. His soul grew still as the view filled an emptiness that had haunted him for so long.

Then a rustle in the branches of the large pine tree behind him caught his attention. He cocked his head, listening as he slowly turned. Something large was hiding in the branches above him. Black bear, or worse, a cougar?

Heart pounding, he thumbed his cowboy hat back on his head, scanning the tree, planning what to do. Run? Stay and stand down whatever wild animal was perched in the tree?

Then he heard a cough just as a backpack fell with a thump to the ground in front of him, followed by an angry exclamation.

"Who's there?" he called out, still feeling that intense jolt of adrenaline surging through his veins.

"Just me," a female voice returned.

The branches rustled again and Lee caught sight of a pair of feet in sandals searching for a branch. Then he saw legs scrabbling for purchase, hands flailing.

A cry of dismay pierced the air and Lee ran closer just as a woman plummeted out of the tree.

He caught her, but they were a tangle of legs and arms as they tumbled to the ground, breaking her fall. A camera, hanging around her neck, swung around and cracked him on the head.

They lay like that a moment as Lee's ears rang and his head throbbed from the impact of the camera.

Finally the woman pushed herself away from him and scrambled to her feet.

Lee blinked as he tried to orient himself. He slowly stood frowning at the woman in front of him, who seemed more concerned about her camera than herself, or him, for that matter.

Her hair was tucked up in a ball cap, and a large pair of sunglasses was perched on a nose sprinkled with freckles. She wore khaki shorts, a white tank top now smeared with dirt and a brown vest with numerous zipped and buttoned pockets. She pulled a cloth out of one of them and was wiping down the body of her camera.

The woman looked familiar, but he couldn't immediately place her.

"Everything okay?" he asked, gingerly touching his forehead. His hand came away tinged with blood, so he pulled a handkerchief out of the back pocket of his blue jeans and dabbed at it.

"I think so," she murmured, tucking the cloth in her chest pocket. "The body looks good, but I'll have to check the inside later."

"I meant with you."

She finally looked up at him and lifted her chin in a defensive move. "Yeah. Sorry about that. I'm fine." She cleared her throat. "You didn't need to catch me, you know. I would have been okay. Are *you* okay?"

"You might have broken a leg," he returned, the sharp pain in his head settling in to a dull ache as he ignored her question. He gestured toward a long red scrape on the inside of her wrist. "You might want to get that looked at, as well. You don't want it to get infected."

She lifted her arm and gave it a cursory glance. "It's fine." She looked back at him. "Looks like you got a nasty cut on your head, though."

"It's fine too."

"Awesome. Blood's streaming down your face, I've got a scrape that is just starting to hurt…but we're both okay." She waggled her fingers as if to make sure they were still functioning, and then she gave him a self-deprecating smile. "Again, sorry about that. I should have been more careful—and I wasn't very grateful for your help."

"Apology accepted." Lee returned her look for look, his own brain trying to place her familiarly beautiful features, or what he could see of her face, half-hidden by the sunglasses. "And at least you're not the bear or cougar I thought you were."

She angled him a mischievous smile as she bent over to pick up the knapsack that had been the first victim. "Didn't think I was old enough to be a cougar."

Too late Lee caught the implied insult he had given her. "No. Sorry, I meant the cat. Mountain lion might have been a better designation."

She smiled again and Lee couldn't stop a twinge of attraction. She was an intriguing combination of pretty and striking.

"Do we know each other?" he asked, trying to tweak out a memory that seemed to elude him.

"I can't believe a good-looking guy like you doesn't have better lines," she quipped as she slipped her camera in her bag.

"Chalk it up to being out of practice," he returned.

"So you decided to practice on me?"

He laughed, surprised at how easy she was to be around for someone he just met. "Sorry. My dad always said clichés are the tool of the lazy mind."

Her answering chuckle as she put her camera back in the knapsack created a tremor of awareness and behind that a flutter of familiarity. Not too many people knew about this place.

Why was she up in the tree and how had she gotten here? No vehicle was parked at the end of the trail.

She stood, slinging the bag over her shoulder, and it seemed she was looking at him, as if she was trying to figure out who *he* was.

Which was precisely what he was doing.

Then, as she pulled her sunglasses off, she knocked her hat off her head and her auburn hair tumbled to her shoulders, her amber eyes fringed with thick lashes were revealed, and reality followed like a Montana snowstorm as things clicked into place.

He knew exactly who she was.

Abby Newton. Daughter of Cornell Newton, the man Lee had run down with his truck after a party that had gotten out of hand. The accident had put Cornell in the hospital and Lee in jail. The shame of what he had done had kept Lee away from home for almost nine years.

Until now.

He knew the precise moment her own recognition of him clicked. She took a step back, her eyes narrowed and her impudent grin morphed into a scowl.

"Well, well," she said, the ice in her voice making him shiver. "Lee Bannister, back from exile. I'm going to blame my slow recollection to the fall out of the tree. Didn't think I'd ever forget your face, but then, you've changed since I last saw you."

"Hey, Abby." He tried to sound casual. Tried to ignore the mockery in her voice.

Lee hadn't seen her since her father was awarded damages of two hundred thousand dollars and he'd been sentenced to three and a half years in prison for reckless driving under the influence. The accident he'd caused had put her father in the hospital and had created injuries that, as far as he knew, Cornell was still dealing with.

That had been over nine years ago. Lee had paid his debt to society and was still working on repaying his parents for the money they had to dole out for the settlement. His father had to downsize his cattle herd as a consequence. When Lee was released from prison, he took on a job working offshore rigs. And he sent his folks every penny he could. He hadn't been home since.

Though Abby was a Saddlebank native as well, he had heard she was working overseas. Seeing her now was a shock and an unwelcome surprise. She reminded him of a past he'd spent years trying to atone for.

"I'm guessing you're back for Keira's wedding," she said, her voice matter-of-fact, settling her hat back on her head and pulling the bill down as if to hide the anger in her gaze.

"And the anniversary celebration," he added gruffly.

The anniversary was a big deal. Refuge Ranch was one of the few family-owned ranches that could trace their ownership back to when settlers first started in the basin. A reporter was even coming to spend time at the ranch and planned to cover the celebrations and do a feature story on it for *Near and Far*.

His father had warned him that he would be the one to help the guy out.

More penance, he thought. Babysitting a reporter and showing him around the ranch.

"Right," she said, tucking her sunglasses in the pocket of her vest. "I heard about that. One hundred and fifty years of Bannisters at Refuge Ranch. Quite the heritage."

Was she mocking him? Though he couldn't blame her if she did. He knew he wasn't her favorite person.

He looked back over his shoulder at the view he had hoped would give him some peace and ease him into a difficult homecoming. He didn't think the past would be dredged up quite so quickly, however.

Help me through this, Lord, he prayed, clinging to the faith he'd returned to during those years in prison. *Help me to accept what I can't change.*

He turned back to Abby, knowing he had to face reality. Trouble was, he wasn't sure what to say or how to say it.

"I know it's too late and I know that words are easy, but I want to tell you that I'm so sorry for what I did to your father," he said. "I wish…I wish I could turn back time. Do it over again."

"You're not the only one who wishes that by any stretch."

The bitterness in her voice made him wait a beat to give the moment some weight.

"My father spent a lot of time struggling with pain," she continued. "He was a broken man after that accident. My parents' marriage couldn't hold together. What you did to my family…me and my brother—" She stopped there, holding up her hand as if trying to halt the memories. "Never mind. Neither of us can change anything. It's done. I shouldn't have said anything."

Lee knew he deserved every bit of her derision, but he would be lying if he said he wasn't hurt by it. At one time Abby had been important to him. Her poor opinion of him had been almost as agonizing as the loss of his freedom.

"I better go," she said quietly. "I need to get back to town."

"How?" he asked, shifting to another topic. "I didn't see a car."

"My friend Louisa has it. Remember her?"

"Of course. You two were joined at the hip in high school."

"Still are, apparently. We live together in Seattle. She's back in Saddlebank visiting her parents and she'll be back soon." Her words were terse and Lee guessed this conversation was over.

"Well, I hope you have a good visit with your mom," he said. "And if I don't see you again, take care."

Her only reply was a curt nod. She gave him a humorless smile, then turned and walked away.

Lee dragged his hand over his face. Well, that awkward meeting was done with.

If he played his cards right, he might not have to see her again, which was fine with him.

She was a reminder of the past he had spent a lot of years trying to atone for.

"Dumb, dumb, dumb," Abby Newton muttered as she strode through the underbrush toward the road, yanking her cell phone out of her pocket. Of all the clumsy, stupid and just plain humiliating things to happen, she had to end up falling out of a tree right on top of Lee Bannister. And then she flirted with him.

She didn't know why her brain had been firing so slowly that it took so long for her to recognize him.

Abby swallowed hard. She blamed it on her own prejudicial memories. This guy looked nothing like the Lee Bannister she had seen swaggering out of the lawyer's office on his way to prison, as if he couldn't care less about destroying her family. That Lee Bannister was a slender young man with shortly cropped hair who wore a perpetual smirk and acted as if the world owed him a favor. He had always been a too-large personality in her life, but for a few months just before graduation, they had dated. She had naively thought she had tamed the wild man. Until she found out about the bet his delinquent friends had made with him about going out with her.

The shame of that could still catch her off guard from time to time.

Now it seemed that Lee's rebellious attitude had morphed into a hardness that seemed bred into his very bones. His shoulders and chest had filled out. His hair was long, dark and framed a face with a strong chin, pronounced cheekbones and eyes enhanced by slashing dark eyebrows. In short, his features held a rugged maturity she suspected came from his time in prison and his years of manual labor after that.

For a heartbeat she felt a glimmer of sympathy.

But all it took was the memory of her father, a broken and hurting man, lying in a hospital bed to remind her that Lee could never pay enough for what he'd done to their family. Her father was a changed man after Lee hit him with his truck, drunk, on his way back from a party.

The alcohol that had impaired Lee's driving had also taken over her father's life. He became an alcoholic, stopped working and spent days in physical pain.

Abby's family was sundered in two when her parents divorced a year after the accident. Cornell left town and she only heard sporadically from him after that, the most recent time being a few weeks ago.

She shook off the dark memories as she strode to the road, punching in her friend's number on her cell phone.

Abby had made her own way in the world in spite of what had happened to her family. She had put Lee and the heartbreak he had caused behind her. As if determined to prove that her life's tragic circumstances were not going to define her, she had graduated from high school and college with honors, and then worked tirelessly to pave a thriving career for herself.

A shiny black pickup truck was parked, askew, just off the highway when she came out of the lane. She suspected it was Lee's. Though it wasn't the candy-apple-red truck his parents had given him in high school—the vehicle that had mowed her father down—it still looked expensive and new.

She shook her head. Some things didn't

change, she thought as she lifted her phone to her ear.

"Can you come and get me?" Abby asked when Louisa answered. She tucked her cell phone between her chin and shoulder as she dug in her backpack for her water bottle. Her mouth was dry, but she suspected that had more to do with the meeting she'd just had than the warmth of the afternoon.

"Did you get some good pictures?" her friend asked.

Abby thought of the breathtaking view, but somehow the satisfaction she had with the photos was tempered by seeing Lee Bannister. Not that she should be totally surprised. She knew she would be crossing paths with him at some time during her visit. Saddlebank was a small town after all.

Truth was, for many years she had imagined her first face-to-face meeting with Lee. But, in her thoughts, that reunion was one where she was aloof, calm and in charge of the situation.

Not falling on top of him and then flirting with him.

She had climbed the tree to get a better panorama shot of the river valley through a break she saw in the pine branches. Though it did net her some great images, in retrospect it might not have been the best decision.

"What's your ETA?" she asked her friend.

Louisa's sigh didn't sound encouraging. "I'm about ten miles out yet. Jaden needed some groceries, so I said I would help him. I was on my way back to you when I got a flat tire. I'm so sorry."

Abby suppressed an angry sigh. When she had pulled over to take some pictures, Louisa asked if she could borrow the car to drop off some things at a friend's place only a mile down the road. Abby wanted to take her time snapping the pictures, so she had agreed. However, Louisa's going all the way to town with her car had *not* been discussed.

"How did you get a flat? I just put new tires on."

"I think I might have run over a nail at Jaden's place. The yard is a junk heap. I just called roadside service," Louisa said. "They can't come for half an hour, though."

"You can't change it yourself?" Abby bit her lip, trying to think what to do. She had told her mother she would be there by four. It was quarter to the hour now.

"Not everyone is as self-sufficient as you, girl."

Abby didn't want to remind her that same self-sufficiency was a by-product of being the oldest child of a family whose father had withdrawn into alcohol. Whose mother's bitterness over their circumstances had caused her to retreat well within herself. The day after her father's accident, much of the responsibility of running the house, taking care of her brother, had fallen on Abby's slender shoulders.

It had eventually taken a toll.

"Okay. I'll see you when I see you. Maybe I can hitch a ride." Abby tried not to get riled up at the idea that Louisa had her car and she had to hitchhike.

Skyline Trail, the name of the road she was heading down, wasn't that busy, but it was a Friday afternoon. Surely someone would be headed to town.

"Again, I'm so sorry," Louisa said.

She seemed to be on the receiving end of a lot of apologies today, Abby thought crossly as she ended the call.

She dropped her phone into one of the pockets of her vest and then pulled her camera out again to check it better. She frowned when she saw the tiny flecks of blood she had missed cleaning off one corner of the camera's body.

Lee's blood.

She stuffed the camera back in her bag. Later. She would deal with that later.

She strode to the road, then stopped, tapping her fingers on her arm trying to figure out what to do. She couldn't sit here and wait, knowing Lee would be coming back out any moment. She'd have to hitch a ride after all. So she slipped the other strap of her backpack over her other arm and started walking, wishing she'd put on her hiking boots.

A light breeze sifted up the road, easing the heat of the sun now beating down on her. The road took a gentle turn and she was once again looking over the basin that cradled Saddlebank and the ranches surrounding it. She stopped and pulled her knapsack off, the photographer in her constantly looking for another angle, the right light as she quickly pulled her camera out. She withdrew her telephoto lens out of her bag just as she heard the growl of a truck starting up.

Lee's truck.

There was no way she was getting a ride from him.

Her history with Lee was even older than the accident. Though that traumatic event had been the lowest point, there had been others. She had been attracted to Lee Bannister most of her life, harboring her secret crush. But Lee was part of a very wild, very cool group. He, David Fortier, son of a neighboring rancher, and Mitch Albon, son of a lawyer in town, ran around together, partying and living recklessly, flirting and teasing girls.

Lee had never paid the slightest attention to her. Then, suddenly, out of the blue, he seemed to notice her. He would chat her up, leaning against the locker beside hers, smiling that slightly mocking smile that always made her weak at the knees. When Lee had, unexpectedly, asked her to the prom, she could hardly believe her luck. Of course she had said yes. He was a senior, she a lowly sophomore. To her surprise, they had a wonderful time. And, even better, they dated a few more times after that.

It seemed too good to believe. Lee Bannister, one of the most eligible guys in the valley, was going out with her. And then it all fell apart. At a party she had attended with Lee, Mitch drew her aside and laughingly told her the truth. David Fortier had made a bet with Lee to take Abby out. It had nothing to do with any kind of attraction—it was a simple joke.

She was crushed and felt degraded. She pulled back from Lee after that, turning down his invitation to come with him to another party knowing David and Mitch would be there. Facing them would be too humiliating. Lee, angry with her, went anyway. And on the way back from that party, her father was struck down by Lee, and her life changed forever. Abby shook off the memories and quickly spun the lens on as she glanced around, looking for a place to hide, the noise from Lee's truck growing louder. The ditch was a broad expanse of grass; the trees on the edge could offer her a hiding place. She snatched up her knapsack and started running.

But the sandals that were unsuitable for a long trek were even more unsuitable for running.

The toe of the sandal caught on a bottle hidden by the grass. She faltered, windmilling her arms, trying to maintain her balance, but gravity and momentum won out over will. Her knapsack flew in one direction, her hat another, and then her foot twisted under her, hit something sharp and she fell, chest down, on the grassy verge. Right on top of her sunglasses.

Of course. Why not?

Abby wanted to laugh and cry at the same time. Two clumsy mishaps in the space of twenty minutes and both in front of the man she wanted to avoid as long as possible.

She lay there a moment, hoping that Lee wouldn't see her sprawled out on the grass. But then his truck slowed and stopped, and when he turned off the ignition, she couldn't hide. So she slowly rose to her feet and then stumbled as pain shot through her leg.

She looked down, dismayed to see blood pouring out of a cut in her ankle. She shifted and saw the culprit. The broken bottle.

Good thing her tetanus shots were up to date.

She reached out for her knapsack, more concerned about the well-being of her camera than her injury.

"You okay?" she heard Lee call out as he came down the ditch toward her.

"I just fell," she said, sucking in a quick breath through her clenched teeth as she dug through her bag to find something to stop the bleeding.

"You're not okay," he muttered, clutching her ankle. "You got anything for this?"

"In my bag. A lens-cleaning cloth."

He was too close. The vague scent of woodsy aftershave and the touch of his hand made her want to pull away. Then Lee bent down beside her and lifted her foot, cradling it in one hand while wrapping the cloth she had given him around it.

His head was inches from hers. His thick brown hair had a slight wave and curled around the collar of his striped shirt. His hands were gentle, but to Abby each touch felt like a brand.

Then he looked up at her, his gaze holding hers, his eyes narrowed. His eyes weren't brown, she thought absently, suddenly feeling as if she couldn't breathe. She saw a hint of bronze in the lines around his iris. His lashes were dark; his eyebrows darker still, meeting like a slash across a narrow nose.

If anything he was even more handsome than she remembered.

"I have a first-aid kit in my truck," he said, turning his attention back to her ankle. "We need to take care of this. Don't move."

"Okay. Sure." She felt angry at her sudden breathlessness, frustrated with her reaction to him. She blamed it on the old, high school emotions he too easily reawakened in her.

As he left she shook her head, the pain in her ankle battling for attention with the humiliation of falling not once, but twice in front of the one man she had hoped to face with some measure of dignity.

With a light sigh she leaned back, closing her eyes against another wave of pain, once again resenting Lee Bannister. If it weren't for meeting him again, she wouldn't have tried to run away.

It's your own fault, her more rational voice reminded her. *You didn't need to act so silly. Like you always acted around him.*

Her cheeks burned as hotly as her hurting ankle as older memories assailed her. Times in high school that she would sit on the sidelines of his football game, pretending she was snapping action pictures of the team for the school yearbook when, in fact, she was trying to get the perfect shot of him to keep for herself.

He destroyed your father's life.

She shook her head as if to put her memories in their proper place and order. Her foolish feelings for her high school crush should have been swept away by his actions both in high school and shortly after graduation.

And yet they hadn't been completely. It was that irony that created an ongoing struggle in her soul. He was the enemy and the first boy she had ever truly cared for all wrapped in one far too appealing package.

Help me, Lord, she prayed. *Help me to put this all in perspective. Help me to keep my head clear until he's gone. He's taken up too much of my thoughts already.*

She winced as she shifted her leg and another shard of pain shot through her ankle, but she reminded herself that she only had to get through the next half hour. Then she would be back with Louisa, and Lee could go back to being a footnote in her life.

He returned with a first-aid kit that he set down on the grass as he knelt down at her feet. Then he opened the tin and looked up at her again.

And her crazy heart did another silly flip.

"You should probably take your sandal off,"

he advised, his deep voice quiet as he rummaged through the first-aid kit.

She nodded, bracing herself as she leaned forward to unbuckle her sandal.

"This will probably hurt," he said, ripping open an antiseptic cloth and dabbing it on the cut once her sandal was removed.

She grimaced and he muttered an apology, but soon the cut was cleaned out. It wasn't deep.

"I don't think you'll need stitches," he murmured. "But you might want to have it looked at anyway." He pulled a bandage out of the first-aid kit.

"I can put that on," she said, reaching for the bandage, but she dropped it when he handed it to her and then it took her a few moments to get the packaging off.

Relax. Settle down, she told herself. But she was all thumbs and managed to paste the bandage to itself.

"Can I?" Lee asked, taking another bandage out of the tin.

Abby wanted to say no, but she was tired of looking clumsy in front of him, so she just nodded.

His hands were large, but his movements were confident and sure. He gently pressed the edges of the bandage down, then lifted his gaze to look at her.

"I hope this doesn't handicap you, he said, sitting back on his heels. "You were in quite a rush to photograph whatever it was you wanted."

She could have pounced on the out he had given her, but for some reason she couldn't lie. "Actually I wasn't running to get a picture. I was trying to hide from you. I thought you would probably stop and offer me a ride…and I didn't want to take you up on it."

A muscle ticked in his jaw. "Well, guess you're stuck with getting a ride from me after all," he said as he helped her to her feet.

Abby leaned over to pick up her backpack and her sandal, not bothering to reply. But he grabbed both before she could. Then he held out his arm to help her, but she hesitated to take it.

"You'll fall again if you don't let me help you," he warned.

Abby saw the wisdom in this, then hooked her arm through his and let him lead her up the hill to his truck, the grass prickling her one bare foot.

She was far too aware of his arm holding her up, him walking alongside her. At one time this would have been a dream come true for her. At another it would have been her worst nightmare and a complete betrayal of everything that had happened to her family.

She closed her eyes, praying once again.

Just get through this, she reminded herself as he helped her into his truck. *Get through this and you won't have to see him again until it's time for you to leave.*

Chapter Two

Lee put the truck in gear, glanced over his shoulder and pulled onto the road.

He looked over at his passenger, but she was bent over, slipping her sandal on and buckling it loosely. They drove in silence for a mile or so and then he stole another glimpse of her. Now she was crouching on her side of the cab, holding her knapsack like a shield.

She clearly would have preferred to be anywhere but in the cab of his truck.

"I'm not a reckless driver anymore," he said, trying not to sound annoyed.

Abby shot him a quick look. "I hope not." She was silent a moment, then lifted her chin, staring directly at him. "It's just that I haven't seen you since that day—"

"That day at the lawyer's," he finished for her. He gazed back at the road again, pressing his lips together as the past, once again, dropped into the present. The night of the accident was a blur to him. He blamed his drinking that night on the fact that he thought Abby, the best thing that had ever happened to him, didn't want to date him. She was supposed to have come to the party with him, but she had phoned and told him not to bother calling her again. Whatever they had going, was over. She didn't tell him why.

All he remembered of that night was dropping his keys on the way out of the party.

The very next memory was of coming to behind the wheel of his truck, which had plowed into a tree, and a police officer asking him if he knew his name.

He suppressed a shudder at the flashbacks that always followed. Being taken away in the cruiser. Finding out that his truck had struck Abby's father before it hit the tree. His parents coming to see him in the jail. The horror and the regret and the twisting guilt. Dealings with the lawyers and the subsequent prison sentence. He relived that night of the party every day for the first year after it happened, wishing he could turn back time.

Part of him wanted to ask Abby why she broke up with him before the party, but given the events that had fragmented their lives, it seemed petty.

"Looks like you're still taking pictures," he remarked, trying to fill the oppressive silence between them. At one time he had cared about her and thought she cared about him. Maybe, in spite of what happened, they could find some point of connection.

"I'm working as a photographer and writer," Abby said after a moment of silence. "Mostly travel pieces for the magazine I work for."

"You enjoy it?" he asked, glancing over at her, then down at her camera.

"It pays the bills," she replied, turning her camera off and slipping it back in her camera bag. She folded her arms over the bag and then winced.

"Do you want anything for the pain?" he asked. "I've got some painkillers in the first-aid kit too."

She shook her head, turning to look out the side window.

Guess the conversation's over. He stared ahead at the road, the thump of the frost heaves, the hum of the tires, the clinking of his key chain against the steering column the only sounds in the truck. Ten more uncomfortable and silent minutes later, they rounded a corner and saw an automobile parked by the side of the road.

"That's my car," Abby said. The vehicle listed

to one side and Lee could see that one tire was flat.

A tall, lanky girl lay on the hood of the car. She lifted her head as Lee parked the truck and then she languorously raised herself off the car when he got out. Lee was surprised as he rounded the hood of his truck. This was Louisa? He remembered a rather plump girl who never made any apology for telling him that Abby was too good for him.

She would be pleased to know she was right.

Abby was already out of the cab and slipping her knapsack over her arm, ignoring him as he offered her his assistance. She hopped, using the truck to balance herself as she made her way to the car.

"What happened to you, girl?" Louisa called out, hurrying to help her friend. "Can't leave you alone a minute before you get into trouble—" Then her voice faded away as a smile curved her lips.

"Hello," she said to him, her smile warm and friendly.

Obviously she didn't recognize him either, Lee noted, thinking of that brief moment when he and Abby were almost flirting with each other at the lookout point.

"Louisa, this is Lee…Bannister," Abby said, looking pointedly at her friend. Louisa's smile fled and her features hardened as she caught Abby by the arm, helping her to the car.

"How did you end up with him?" Louisa hissed, loud enough for Lee to hear.

Him. How quickly he had been dismissed. He shouldn't have expected anything different, though. Louisa had made no secret of what she thought of him in high school, and he didn't imagine the events following the prom had enhanced his standing with Abby's friend.

"I cut my ankle and Lee helped me out," Abby said, her voice strained. Lee felt sorry for her. She sounded as though the pain was getting worse.

"How did you cut your ankle, girlfriend?"

Abby waved off Louisa's questions. "Just help me to the car so I can sit while we wait for the guy to come."

"What guy?" Lee asked.

"Someone from Alan's garage," Louisa said in a dismissive tone. "He's going to change the tire."

"I can do that," Lee offered.

Louisa and Abby both shot him a surprised look.

"I'm not completely helpless," Lee muttered, walking to the back of the car to check on the tire. It was well and truly flat. "Where's the spare?"

"You don't need to—"

"Alan can do it—"

Abby and Louisa spoke at the same time. Lee almost felt insulted, but he guessed neither of them wanted to spend any more time with him than they had to.

"There's no way I'm leaving you two here stranded," he said, ignoring their protests. "So, where's the spare tire?"

He saw Abby give Louisa another quick look, as if to verify what she should do. "It's in the trunk. Under the carpet. There's a toolbox there, as well." Abby hit the key fob, he heard a click and he opened the trunk.

"I'll help you," she said, hobbling over to his side.

"Go sit on the side of the road," he said. "I don't want you falling again."

The "again" slipped out. The grimace on Abby's face indicated he'd hit a sensitive spot. He imagined that, after first falling out of a tree, then stumbling and getting cut while trying to avoid him, she'd had her share of humiliation. He didn't need to rub it in.

Lee sighed wearily. He clearly wasn't gaining ground with her, so he turned his attention to changing the tire. This he was halfway competent with. He found the spare tire, jack and tools he needed.

While he jacked and loosened nuts, Abby and

Louisa had both taken his advice and sat on the side of the road, talking quietly.

Fifteen minutes later he dumped the flat tire in the back of the car and slammed the trunk shut. "It's ready to go," he said, brushing his hands on his jeans.

Louisa stood, helping Abby to her feet. "What do we owe you?" Louisa asked.

"Nothing. Just being neighborly."

"I prefer to pay you," Abby said, digging in her backpack.

"I prefer you don't." Lee took a step toward his truck. "You'll want to bring that tire in to Alan's to get it fixed. He can swap it for the spare. And, as I mentioned before, you should get that ankle looked at."

"I'll do that." Abby clutched her backpack. "And thanks again for your help and…the ride."

"Okay." Another uncomfortable pause followed. There was nothing more to say or do, so he gave her a tense smile, then walked back to the truck.

As he drove away, he glanced in the rearview mirror, surprised to feel his heart banging against his rib cage.

It was just reaction, he told himself as he sucked in a breath and looked ahead. He wasn't sure if he'd see Abby again, and it didn't matter.

She didn't want to have anything to do with him, and he didn't blame her.

That much hadn't changed.

"You going to tell your mom that you met up with Lee?"

Abby looked up from her camera, glancing ahead at the road as Louisa turned the car around, headed back to Saddlebank. "It's not like I snuck out to see him," she said, wishing she didn't sound so defensive. "It was a rotten coincidence that we both ended up at the same place at the same time."

"Must have been hard for you."

Abby let the sentence settle, contemplating the intricate ebb and flow of feelings that Lee Bannister stirred in her.

It bothered her that she found him even more attractive than she had in high school. She should despise him. He had not only injured her father, but had humiliated her. So, for all intents and purposes, she should feel nothing but contempt for him.

And yet, as she looked down at her camera again, she was annoyed to feel a prickle of tears. It had been nine years since her father's accident. Surely seeing Lee shouldn't bring all this up again. She blamed her wavering emotions on embarrassment. On the fatigue that had dogged her for the past four years, travelling around the world doing pieces on resorts for the travel magazine she worked for. It was a dream job and had paid her enough to set a bunch of money aside. But a weariness and a soul-deep dissatisfaction she couldn't explain seemed to vex her every time she booked another airplane ticket. Every time she checked into a motel.

So she took a month off and, when she still felt the same, asked for an extension. It had taken a lot of wrangling with her editor, but Abby wanted to come home. She hadn't been back in Saddlebank for years. Still, she should have timed her visit better, she realized, and returned after the Bannister anniversary and wedding.

"I knew he was coming back," Abby said finally. "I thought I could avoid him but it seems God has an ironic sense of humor."

"I wouldn't call seeing that rat fink unexpectedly *funny*," Louisa scoffed.

"You might have if you had seen the array of my various falls in front of him. I would have gotten at least an 8.6 for artistic impression."

"And a ten for pain and suffering."

"It's not that bad," Abby said, glancing down at the large bandage Lee had put on her cut.

"Well, that will certainly put a wrinkle in your hiking plans."

Abby had hoped to head up into the high country and take some photos while she was here. Lately she'd been doing some freelance work, selling some of the pictures she took between jobs. She hoped to supplement her income doing her own work and slowly wean herself from the travel pieces she had been doing. "I'll manage."

Louisa was quiet a moment, then turned to her, eyebrows lifted. "So, was it hard to see Lee again?"

"Wasn't easy. The guy has taken up too much space in my brain in the past few years." Abby thought she had erased the shadow he cast on her life. But one look at him and all the tangled emotions twisted her inside out again. "Truth is, I just hate how much influence he's had in my life," she continued. "I feel like I've invested way too much energy in this nonrelationship. And I hope Mom doesn't want to talk about it like she does each time I call her."

"That's probably part of your problem, as well," Louisa said. "She keeps rehashing the same old stuff. Every time I speak with her, it's also all she can talk about. She needs to get past it too."

"It was a hard time for her. Watching Dad suffer and then become this completely different person, then their divorce…" Abby eased out a sigh and shook her head. "It changed our lives."

"I know. I'm not going to lie—seeing Lee was a shock to me too. I'm still ticked at him for what he did to you at the prom. Taking you out on a bet from those louses he hung around with."

"That was even longer ago," Abby said with a snicker.

"Maybe, but I think that was almost as hard for you as the accident." Louisa grew pensive, staring at the road ahead, her fingers tapping the steering wheel.

Abby was about to reply to that when she heard the muffled trill of her cell phone. She grabbed her backpack, recognizing the ring tone she had assigned to her editor. What could Maddie possibly want now?

"Let it ring," Louisa snorted. "You're on holiday."

But Abby had never been able to let a phone ring; the insistent tone always created an urgency she couldn't ignore. Besides, she was fully aware of how much she owed her editor right now. Abby had turned down two assignments so that she could extend her vacation.

"Hey, Maddie. What can I do for you?" she said, setting her camera aside.

"You in Montana? Close to home like you said you'd be?"

"Yeah. I'm coming up to Saddlebank in a couple of minutes."

"Awesome. So listen up…I need your help. Badly. I need you to do me a favor."

A knot settled in the pit of her stomach. It was never simply a favor with Maddie. On the contrary, it was always a huge, huge favor.

"Burt Templeton was supposed to do that Montana piece, but he's stuck in Bangkok," Maddie was saying. "Got some kind of weird tropical virus. He's getting transferred to a hospital in Portland tomorrow, but he's officially out of commission for another couple of weeks." She huffed out a breath. "Which leaves me royally stuck. It's not far from your hometown, and won't take a lot of time. Four days, maybe five or six max. It's a puff piece, Abby. Pictures. Some interviews. Please help me out?"

Abby was already shaking her head no. She was fairly sure she knew which piece Maddie was talking about.

"I hate to do this, but I'm desperate," Maddie insisted. "So I'm calling in my favor…" And there it was. The favor her editor kept threatening to use when Abby had asked for all this time off. Abby knew she owed Maddie a lot, especially the past few months. When Abby first started, she hadn't been completely straight up with Maddie, letting the editor think she knew more about feature writing than she did, but thankfully Maddie saw her potential. She'd been a patient and encouraging editor, pushing Abby to see situations differently. To think outside the box. To go beyond clichés, not only in her writing but her photography, as well. And during the past half year, as Abby felt the burnout of the work, she'd also extended a number of deadlines for Abby.

"Is it that piece on the Bannister ranch?" she asked hesitantly.

"Yeah, it is. The one you turned down."

And for a good reason, Abby thought, her heart dropping like a stone.

"Sorry, Maddie. I couldn't do it then…and I can't do it now."

"You can't back out on me, missy. You know you owe me." Maddie built on her advantage. "I wouldn't play this card if I didn't have a reason, and right now I'm stuck."

"And there's no one else?" Abby asked, clinging to her last shred of hope.

"No. And I'm asking you because you know Montana. You'll see things no one else would notice. You'll have a unique take on the story."

And wasn't that the truth?

Abby pressed a finger to her temple as the

too-familiar ache began making itself known. She wanted to say no. Wanted to protest that she couldn't do this, but she had already said yes. And she owed her editor.

"Okay. Send me the particulars, and I'll see what I can come up with."

"Great. Consider it done. Email me an outline ASAP and we'll take it from there."

Abby ended the call, trying to calm her pounding heart.

"You look like someone just punched you in the stomach," Louisa said as she slowed to make the turn into town. "You get fired?"

"No. I just got a job."

"That's good, I guess. Though you are technically on holiday." She glanced over at her. "So, what's the piece?"

"It's on Refuge Ranch's hundred and fiftieth anniversary."

"You can't be serious!" Louisa's exclamation of dismay eerily echoed Abby's own feelings. "Say no. You've got to say no."

Abby squeezed her now-trembling hands between her knees to steady them. "I can't. I owe my editor more than I can ever repay. Besides, it's just a job."

"It's more than that and you know it. What will your mother think?"

"That I shouldn't do this." Abby laid her head

back on the headrest, the weariness clinging to her the past few months growing stronger. She felt unsatisfied, unfulfilled. It seemed every day was a struggle to get through, and her extended hiatus hadn't eased that feeling away. If anything, it had become worse.

"I don't know. Maybe I *should* do this," she said softly. "Like I said before, this whole thing with Lee and my dad has taken up too much of my thoughts. I think it's because, before today, I hadn't seen Lee since the sentencing, let alone talk with him. Maybe if I spend some time with him, on his ranch, it will help put things in perspective."

"Can't see how that's a good idea," Louisa warned. "I doubt your mother would appreciate you working with the enemy, so to speak."

"She might not, but I don't think I have much choice." Abby sorted through her thoughts, trying to find the right motivation for what she had just agreed to. "For the past year I've been praying to find a way to get some closure on everything that happened. This might be my chance."

"Maybe, but I hope this doesn't make things worse for you," Louisa replied.

Abby shrugged as the familiar buildings of the town she had grown up in slipped past the window, each one bringing back a myriad of memories. Some good. Some not.

She sincerely hoped taking on this assignment would help her finally put Lee Bannister and all that he had done in her life behind her.

Chapter Three

"I'm so blessed. All my children home at one time," Ellen Bannister said, folding her hands, looking over at Lee, who was already sitting down at the dinner table. "And soon Tanner will be a part of this family." She beamed at Tanner, Keira's fiancé, and Heather and her fiancé, John, who were also seated with them.

As Lee caught her loving glance, he couldn't help but agree. Though he'd been back to the ranch a few times since he left, either Heather or Keira had been gone when he'd been here and vice versa. Now, for the first time in years, they were all gathered together at once.

"The family is growing," Lee mused.

"We're doing our part," Heather said, the rich scent of a roast beef wafting through the dining room as she set a large steaming platter of sliced meat on the table beside the salads.

"You need to catch up, mister," John quipped, giving Heather a wink as she sat down beside him.

"I don't know about that," Lee said. "You guys are a tough act to follow."

John with his blond hair and chiseled features was the perfect match for his sister, Heather, a stunning former model who was always looking picture-perfect.

"I know you'll have a hard time finding someone as glamorous as my future wife," John returned with a laugh as he let his arm rest across Heather's shoulders. "But I have faith in you. You never seemed to have any trouble in high school getting the girls."

Unbidden came a picture of Abby with her pretty auburn hair and her sprinkling of freckles.

He shook his head as if to rid himself of the notion, getting up to take one of the bowls his sister Keira was carrying into the dining room. He sniffed as he put it on the table. "Ginger-glazed carrots. You read my mind. These from the garden?"

"You bet," Keira said, setting a bowl of baby potatoes beside it. "We might have been premature picking them, though. None of them are very big."

"I'll say," Tanner put in, pulling a chair out

for his future wife. His dark hair, brown eyes and dark eyebrows gave him a hard look, but Lee knew the former bronc rider was a softie when it came to his sister. He also knew Tanner was the complete opposite of his deceased brother, David Fortier, Lee's former friend. "We had to dig up a quarter of a row of carrots and four potato plants before we got enough for supper."

"It'll be worth it," Keira said, brushing her blond locks off her face. Her green eyes sparkled with humor as she sat down beside Tanner, flashing him a loving smile.

"I'll say it was. This looks and smells amazing," Lee raved, his stomach growling.

He hadn't eaten since that single granola bar he'd grabbed at a gas station on his way up here. A combination of nerves and excitement at coming home had made it hard for him to eat. And after he'd met Abby Newton, any appetite he might have had faded away. Her veiled antagonism stuck in his throat, and he still cringed at the memory. He knew he would be facing the shadows of the past coming back to the ranch, but he didn't think those shadows would take the form of actually encountering Abby so soon.

"So, where's Adana?" he asked, finally realizing that John's daughter wasn't with them.

"She's with Sandy's parents," John said.

"They wanted to take her to put some flowers on Sandy's grave."

"That's pretty heavy for a two-year-old to deal with," Lee remarked.

John shrugged. "Sandy was their only daughter. They don't want Adana to forget her."

Silence followed that pronouncement. John had been married to Sandy for two years before she died giving birth to Adana. Sandy's parents still lived in Saddlebank and, from what Lee understood, took care of Adana from time to time.

"And that's only right," Ellen said finally. "I like to think my children would remember me if something happened."

"Something already did," Monty said, referring to the break in her neck Ellen had suffered over half a year ago. "And thank the good Lord you made it through that."

Guilt suffused Lee at the thought that his mother had gone through all that pain while he stayed away.

"And thank the good Lord that the brace came off in time for Keira's wedding," Ellen said brightly. "I would have a hard time finding a mother of the bride outfit wearing that silly thing."

"You'd look good no matter what you wore," Monty murmured, patting her on the arm.

Lee couldn't stop a tinge of envy at his family's obvious happiness. Though he knew both his sisters had had their trials in the past, they had overcome them and had found happiness and someone who loved and accepted them exactly as they were.

He hadn't had the same experience. Abby had been the last woman he was serious about. Then it was prison and after that, trying to find work. He had tried dating but couldn't seem to connect with anyone who he wanted to spend time with. Of course, once any decent woman heard about his prison term, she seemed to back off.

"I think we can get started," Monty said. "Like you said, Ellen, we are richly blessed. A wedding coming up next week, the anniversary celebrations and all our children home."

Then he bowed his head and thanked the Lord for the food, for their family and the many blessings they'd received over the years. He prayed for strength and for wisdom and thanked the Lord for his sacrificial love.

When he said amen, Lee kept his head bent a moment longer, letting the prayer soak into his weary soul. The offshore drilling rig work he'd been doing—camp jobs and being on the road for weeks at a time—didn't allow for much faith community. And he truly missed being a part of a robust spiritual life.

He lifted his head to catch his father looking

at him, a pensive expression on his face as if he guessed where Lee's mind had been wandering. Then his sisters started chatting, people started passing bowls and plates and he was drawn into the give and take of family conversation and dinner around the Bannister table.

For the first few moments, Lee was more spectator than participant. Other than the two years she'd worked in Seattle, Keira had stayed at Refuge Ranch working with their father, Monty, at his leather-working business, expanding it and putting her own mark on it. Heather had returned this spring and was settling into her work, teaching barrel-racing clinics. John had bought in to the ranch, and he and Heather were making plans to build an arena so she could train horses right on the ranch. Their lives were entwined with the daily rhythm of ranch life.

Lee envied them the peace that suffused their lives. But he had grown up on the ranch as well, understood the language and the way of life, so he was soon drawn into the conversation as the topics moved to pasture management, maximizing profits and alternative feeding methods.

An hour later, after dessert and coffee, Lee sat back in his chair, replete.

"I haven't been this stuffed in a long time,"

he said, rubbing his stomach. "I'm sure I gained six pounds tonight."

"Three helpings of apple pie probably didn't help," Keira teased.

"That's the best apple pie I've had since I left here," Lee said with a groan.

"Guess we'll have to add apple pie to the wedding menu." Tanner grinned at Keira. "Cheesecake and trifle might not be enough for your brother."

Everyone laughed at that, and Lee was about to make a rebuttal when the phone rang.

Monty got up to answer and Heather started clearing the table. Lee stood to help her and as they passed Monty, who was still talking on the phone, his father shot Lee a troubled glance.

"Well, if that's the way it's gotta go, doesn't seem to be much I can do about it," Monty said, scratching his forehead with one finger. He said goodbye and then set the phone back in its cradle.

"What was that about?" Lee asked as he set the plates by the dishwasher.

"That was the editor of the magazine doing the piece on the ranch." Monty crossed his arms over his chest as he leaned back against the counter behind him. "Apparently the guy that was supposed to do the story on the ranch won't be coming."

"Oh no," Heather said. "And you were so excited about having that feature done."

"Does that mean I'm off the hook?" Lee asked. Since everyone else was tied up with preparations for the wedding, he had been volunteered to show the reporter around. Take him on a few rides up in the hills and show him as much of the ranch as he could. They had planned a cattle drive for the cows and calves they had to move to pasture, and had even talked about a campfire out in the hills like the way they used to do during fall roundup.

Monty settled his gaze on Lee, who felt a shiver of apprehension at the concern on his father's face. "The editor, Maddie, found someone else to do the story." He paused and the shiver became a chill. "Abby Newton will be coming tomorrow. She's the reporter slash photographer who is replacing Burt."

Abby took her foot off the accelerator as her car crested the hill leading down into Refuge Ranch, its many buildings clustered in the basin below her. The sprawling ranch house sat off to one side tucked into a copse of spruce. Its large stone chimney soaring skyward from the house was framed by large panes of glass overlooking mountains cradling the basin.

There was another smaller house to the left

of that. From the information Maddie had forwarded her, she suspected that was John Argall's house, the new partner in the ranch. A large shed housing some tractors and haying equipment dominated the rest of the yard. Beside that was another barn and various outbuildings, one of which sported a sign, swinging from a wrought-iron frame. Abby couldn't read the writing from here, but she suspected the building was the leather-working shop where Keira Bannister toiled away. Large corrals took up a few more acres of space, and beyond that pastures rolled away for endless miles. Though it wasn't operating at capacity—Monty had downsized after Lee left—it was still a large ranch. And the Bannister name was embedded in Saddlebank history.

Part of her wanted to turn, run back and tell Maddie she couldn't do this.

How could she deliberately spend time with Lee? Or face the family she insisted pay for what had happened to her father?

But she had said yes, and Abby wasn't someone who went back on her word.

Ever.

So she tamped down the anxiety, stepped on the gas and headed down to Refuge Ranch.

As she got closer to the ranch, she saw a tall, solitary figure leaving the house, head covered by a brown cowboy hat. He looked up when she pulled into the graveled parking pad by the main house. Dark eyes narrowed as he stared in her direction, his hands dropping on his hips, and she guessed Lee was as happy to see her as she was to see him.

No turning back now.

Abby parked her car and turned it off, whispering a quick prayer for strength and courage. Then she grabbed her knapsack and stepped out. She limped to the back door and pulled out a crutch, willing the flush that was even now heating her cheeks to go away. It was embarrassing to need a crutch, but the doctor she had seen last night recommended it for today. Just to make sure the cut healed properly.

"Good morning, Lee," she said as she hobbled toward him.

"Morning." He glanced from her crutch to her. "How's the ankle?"

"Not as bad as yesterday but not as good as the day before. Thankfully the doctor said I could keep it." Then to deflect the attention from herself, she glanced up at his forehead, still sporting a bandage. "How's the head?"

He reached up and touched the bandage. "Oh yeah. It's fine."

"No permanent damage?" The saucy tone in her voice was a defense mechanism, but she could tell from his frown that he didn't appreciate her attempt at levity.

"I think I'll live," he returned. "But that's only my opinion. Head injury patients aren't always reliable."

His comeback surprised her. He was still frowning, but maybe that was his default expression.

"I might have to verify that statement with your other family members." *Seriously, quit already*, she told herself. She always started joking when she was nervous.

He simply nodded and one of those now-too-familiar awkward silences fell between them.

"So, I heard you're doing the piece for the *Near and Far*?" he said.

"Burt contracted some exotic bug and is stuck in a hospital in Bangkok." Which, right about now, sounded more appealing than being stuck in Saddlebank, Montana. "My editor asked me to take over. I happened to be here, so it makes sense. Kind of." She slipped her knapsack over one shoulder and grabbed her crutch. "So… maybe you can bring me to see your father? The sooner I get going, the sooner I can be done."

And didn't that sound enthusiastic.

"I mean, the sooner I can get out of your hair," she amended. "I know you and your family must be busy with all the wedding and ranch celebrations."

Lee sent her a bemused look. "I'm actually kind of useless with canapés and centerpieces. So I'm stuck on writer detail."

"Excuse me…?" she stammered. "What… what do you mean?"

"Dad's busy getting stuff sorted for the anniversary, John, Keira and Heather are all tied up with the wedding and our hired hand's mother ended up in the hospital, so he's had to drop everything to be with her. Which leaves me to show you around."

Abby's poor overworked heart dropped like a rock down a mine shaft.

"I may not have been around the ranch much the last few years, but I know its history," Lee continued, obviously misreading her reaction.

As he talked Abby could only stare at him, feeling just this side of coherent as his words slowly registered. Lee. Would be her guide.

Lee Bannister the man—

She gave herself a mental shake, yanking her foolish thoughts from the past as she struggled to become the professional journalist she was getting paid to be.

"Okay… We'll, uh, work through this."

This bumbling confession netted her another scowl.

"So, I guess this is the home place?" she asked, gesturing toward the ranch house. She'd read the background notes that Maddie had sent her from Burt, but they were scattered bits and pieces of useless information. She was virtually starting from scratch.

"Yes, but it's not the site of the first house," Lee replied. "I can show you the original homestead. It was set closer to the road. Would you like to see it?"

"Of course."

He lifted a dark eyebrow. "You going to be able to walk? It's down the road a couple hundred feet."

"I'll manage," she said, because she had no other choice. Maddie had warned her that she would be doing a lot of traipsing around, possibly even riding. Her ankle didn't hurt as much as yesterday, but she didn't want the cut to open up again. The last thing she needed was another painfully awkward first-aid situation.

"I have an idea of how to make this work. Just wait here," he said, pointing to a wooden bench with pots of brightly colored flowers nestled up against it. "I'll be right back."

She was about to tell him that it didn't matter, but he was already jogging away from her. He ducked into a large building beside the hip-roof barn. A few moments later, a large overhead door rattled open and Lee came putt-putting out of the garage, driving an all-terrain vehicle.

She had to chuckle at the sight of this large, strapping cowboy operating what her brother always referred to as a quad. It didn't look right. Nevertheless, he drove the vehicle up to her and, leaving it running, climbed off.

"Not going to lie, I'm a little disillusioned," she said. "I figured a cowboy like you wouldn't go anywhere on the ranch but astride a horse."

"Quicker to start a quad than head out into the horse pasture to get a horse for such a short trip," he returned, not even cracking a smile. "I'll help you on."

He held out his hand, but she ignored him.

"I think I can manage," she said. She had been on many modes of transportation in her travels, but this would be her first quad ride. The seat looked large enough for the two of them, but she guessed it would mean sitting astride, right behind Lee.

Deal with that later, she thought, trying to figure out how she was going to get on the thing with her injured ankle.

Slow it down and break it down, she told herself. She'd made a fool of herself plenty already in front of Lee because of her tendency toward impulsive behavior. No sense in carrying on the tradition.

First she shrugged off her backpack and set that in the box fixed to a rack across the back of the quad. Then, putting her weight on her good foot and using her crutch for balance, she managed to get her bandaged foot up and over the seat. She shifted her weight, pulled up her crutch and…voilà! She was on.

With no falling whatsoever. Always a good thing.

Lee dropped onto the seat, hit a button on the handlebar and the quad lurched ahead. She caught herself in time, but her grip on the seat was precarious.

"The field's a bit rough, so brace yourself," he cautioned as he flicked the quad into the next gear up.

Rough was an understatement, Abby thought as the quad jostled and bounced over ruts in the field that she suspected were from a tractor. But the worst part of all was that every rut they hit made the quad bounce, had her bumping up against Lee.

She wondered if he had done this on purpose, but when she saw him move forward on the seat, as if to avoid her, she guessed this was a decision he regretted, as well. A few more bounces later, he stopped and turned the quad off.

He quickly dismounted but stayed beside the vehicle while she got off. Then he grabbed her crutch and handed it to her, and while she fitted it under her arm, she forgot her earlier reminder to take her time and she stumbled. He caught her, steadying her, his hand warm on her upper arm.

Abby jerked back, but she almost lost her balance again. This time Lee caught her with both hands.

They stood that way a moment, Abby wishing, praying, she could stop the blush that she knew made her cheeks flame.

"Please let me go," she whispered.

"I will if you promise not to act so jittery. You're going to fall again."

"I'm not jittery," she retorted, tossing her hair back and lifting her chin as if to face him down.

His dark eyes held hers, his expression serious.

"I think you are," he said quietly.

Abby suddenly found herself unable to speak as their gazes locked. The faintest whisper of a breeze rose, cooling her heated cheeks, toying with her hair.

Lee finally released her, then heaved out a sigh. "Look, I know things are weird between us. I get it. But right now I have to help you with this story. I don't like the idea either, but we gotta find a way to work together without being uncomfortable. Put what happened behind us and move on."

Annoyance flickered through her at the seeming control he had of his emotions. Behind that came anger. As if he could simply put behind them what had happened. He was talking about more than something as innocuous as hurt feelings. But on the one hand he was right. Better to address the unpleasantness and get it out of the way than dance around it.

"I'm sure we can do that," she conceded.

He gave her a quick nod of acknowledgment, but when he turned away from her to retrieve her backpack, she also knew her feelings toward Lee wouldn't disappear simply because she wished they would.

They were too complex and too deeply ingrained.

She just hoped she could maintain a semblance of civility with him and not let old memories of her silly schoolgirl crush supersede the reality of what he had done to her family.

Chapter Four

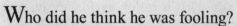

Who did he think he was fooling?

Lee clutched the padded backpack Abby had set on the back of the quad, taking a few seconds to contain himself. The tension between him and Abby was almost thick enough to see. So, obviously, his little speech about moving past what had happened between them wasn't changing anything.

But at least he had gotten it out in the open. They wouldn't have to pretend the pain and uncertainty weren't there.

"I'll take my backpack, please," Abby said as Lee slipped the one strap over his shoulder.

"I don't mind carrying it. I'm afraid it will throw you off balance in this high grass."

"Those cameras and lenses in there are my livelihood," she informed him, her hand still out. "I have never entrusted that backpack to anyone before."

He wanted to protest, not sure he should risk helping her again if she stumbled, but she seemed adamant, so he reluctantly handed the bag over to her. He shoved his hands in his back pocket so he wouldn't be tempted to rush to her rescue again.

That moment, when he had held her arms, it was as if something electric surged between them. He blamed his reaction to the heightened feelings she created in him all across the board. It was just their history that made him so aware of her, but for both their sakes, he knew he had to find a way to keep a tight lid on his emotions. Otherwise this whole arrangement could become untenable.

Lee slowed his steps to match her pace and when they came to a depression in the ground, he stopped.

"Don't know if you can make it out from here, but that's what's left of the first foundation of the house that my great-great-grandfather Cecil Bannister built."

"Is it a darker color?" she asked, pointing to the mounded rectangle in the grass.

"It is. My grandfather used sod from a field closer to the river for the foundation. Different grass type, that's why it shows up."

"A soddy house, I'm guessing?"

"When Grandpa Cecil and his wife came here in 1865, they stayed with a single man who lived a ways down the road. Apparently he was a head case, so Cecil decided he needed to get out as soon as possible. So he built the sod house. It was a quick shelter for them." He spared her a look. "When I was growing up we would come up here for a picnic at least once a year, as if to remind us of the ranch's humble beginnings. When Heather came into the family, this was one of the first places we took her."

"Heather was adopted, wasn't she?"

He nodded slowly. "She was ten when she came into our family."

"I vaguely remember that. Must have been hard for her."

"It was. But she had come from a bad situation. Her mother pretty much neglected her. But she loved the horses…and me and Keira and John took her riding whenever we could. It was the best therapy for her, apparently. It helped her settle in here."

"There is something about the outside of a horse that is good for the inside of a man," Abby said quietly.

He shot her a quick glance. "You know that quote?"

"I know lots of quotes. They rattle around in

my brain, taking up space, waiting for the right opportunity to get hauled out," Abby quipped.

"Well, my dad would say it whenever we were out riding the hills, checking cows and pasture, and he was right." In fact, Lee had hoped to go riding this morning, to reconnect with the land and his legacy, but then he heard Abby was coming. This afternoon, he thought, turning to look at the valley below. The hills called to him and seemed to soothe the restless wandering that defined his life the past couple of years.

"I can see why your great-great-grandfather built up here. It's a beautiful view," Abby murmured as she looked in the same direction.

"It gets windy up here. And when those sod walls dried out, not so good for the relationship between Cecil and Betty, apparently."

"Betty being your many times great-grandmother?"

Lee nodded, drawing in a cleansing breath of the fresh mountain air.

He heard the distinctive click of Abby's camera and glanced over his shoulder to see her with her crutch under her one arm as she took pictures of the foundation. She looped the camera around her neck and made her way to the far side of the old foundation and lifted her camera again.

Lee stepped aside to get out of the picture.

"No, stay there," she said. "But with your back to me."

He did so reluctantly, hands on his hips, feeling suddenly self-conscious. Though he was looking out at the view that he had so missed while he was gone, his attention was focused on the woman behind him, taking picture after picture, her camera beeping, clicking and whirring.

"Are you done yet?"

"Just keep looking away," she ordered.

"You've gotten bossy," he grumbled, but he did what she told him to.

"I've learned a few lessons while traveling overseas," she said. "Dealing with reluctant clients and shy subjects. And some belligerent ones."

He allowed her a few more photographs, her comment about belligerent subjects making him stay where he was. After a while, however, he was done with this.

"So I thought I could show you the current yard site now." He turned and walked toward her.

She took a few more photos, then paused, her camera still in front of her face. A cloud passed over the sun and her camera click-clicked again. "That's perfect," she breathed. "Just perfect."

She unlooped her camera from around her

neck, snapped the lens cap on and slipped the camera in her bag.

"Can we stop halfway down?" she asked. "I'd like to get some different angles of the yard."

"Your wish is my command." He gave her a mocking salute, pleased to see a faint smile tease her lips as he started up the quad. He hadn't seen her smile since she discovered who he was. For a brief moment up at the lookout point, he'd seen her natural and unreserved. He wished he could see that part of her again.

He stopped halfway down the hill as she asked, but this time he stayed on the vehicle while she walked to a hummock, sat down and took a bunch more photos.

Then she looked at the back screen of the camera, adjusted a few settings, took a few more.

The only sounds were from Abby's camera and the occasional lowing of cows from one of the pastures closer to the ranch. John, his father and Nick had moved the cattle a couple of months ago and had figured on moving them to the next pasture when Burt was here to do the anniversary piece.

Lee glanced over at Abby, wondering if she would be willing and/or able to come along on a cattle drive. His mouth quirked. Somehow he couldn't imagine her on the back of a horse.

He was about to look away when she glanced over at him. Their eyes met and it took mere seconds to return to that breathless place of a few moments ago when he had steadied her. Then Abby averted her gaze and Lee gave himself a mental smack.

She's here to do a job and you're here to help her, he reminded himself, folding his arms over his chest. *After that you're both heading back to whatever it was you have to head back to.*

"And how was your day at the Bannister place?" Abby's mother asked, setting a plate of spaghetti in front of her.

Ivy Newton had always been slender, but the past few years had not been kind to Abby's mom. Though her makeup was still impeccable, and her steel-gray hair fashionably styled in a trim pageboy, it wasn't hard to see how time and the events of the past few years had taken their toll. Her cheeks were gaunt and her eyes dull, and once again Abby felt the guilt that always nagged at her when she thought of all her mother had lost after her father's accident. Instead of spending her days taking care of the lovely home they had built up on the hill, puttering in their extensive gardens, her mother now held a job as the manager of the produce department of Saddlebank Market Goods.

"It was okay" was all she could say. Truth was, she wasn't sure herself what to think of the day.

After Lee had brought her down from the original homestead, he showed her the house, yard and barns, giving her background information at each site. It had been a lot to absorb.

And from Lee's account, it was evident he had shown her only a small portion of the Bannister wealth. Hard not to compare the palatial house she had only seen from the outside with the modest apartment her mother now lived in. Though the table and chairs she and her mother sat at were the same elegant set Ivy had been so proud to purchase, and the leather couch, love seat and hand-hooked rug were remnants of a more prosperous life, they looked out of place crammed in the small and somewhat dingy rooms.

Her mother sat down across from her, unfolding her napkin and setting it on her lap. "Spending the afternoon out there probably gave you enough for your piece?"

"I wish. I just got the basics. I gathered, from Maddie, that Burt had figured on spending over a week at the ranch, so I better figure on the same. On top of that, Maddie expects me to attend the actual anniversary celebrations."

Her mother's thinned lips didn't bode well

for pleasant dinner conversation. "When you told me you were coming back home, I never thought you would be spending time with the Bannisters." She spoke their name as if she were talking about a communicable disease. "Especially not with that Lee fellow."

"I'm not thrilled about it either," Abby said, restraining her own frustration. Sure, she didn't like the idea of being with Lee every day, but she had to treat this like any other job. Her mother's obvious antagonism wasn't going to make being dispassionate about it any easier. "I'll be home every night and you're working all day anyway," she added in her defense.

"You're right, of course. It's just…"

"Awkward. I know."

"Just get through it," her mother said. "It will be over soon enough." Then she folded her hands and lowered her head to pray a blessing over the food.

"Thank you, Lord, for this food you have blessed us with," she prayed. "May it nourish our bodies. Forgive our sins. Be with the poor, the sick and the needy. Amen."

Abby couldn't help a slight smile as she kept her head bowed a moment longer. The prayer was the same one her mother had prayed over every meal as long as she could remember. Abby's own prayers had always been a snarled mixture of petitions and frustration and fear. After her father's accident, they centered on her anger with Lee Bannister and the changes his actions inflicted on her family. But all through the family's struggles, her mother's simple prayer remained steadfastly the same.

"And how was *your* day?" Abby asked, picking up her fork.

"The usual. Keith McCauley was complaining about the grapes we brought in, when I think he was really grumping about the fact that his daughters don't come visit him anymore." Her mother huffed lightly. "Can't help but feel bad for the man. He's so lonely. Plus I think he misses being sheriff."

"His daughters stayed at the ranch over the summer months, didn't they?" Abby asked, vaguely remembering seeing three young girls sitting with Mr. McCauley in church on Sundays from June to the end of August.

"They did. Until each of them turned eighteen. Then they stopped." Ivy wiped her mouth and took a drink of water. "Kind of like your little brother."

Abby didn't reply. She knew embedded in the comment about Elliot was a tiny barb directed her way. The same reasons that kept Elliot teaching at a secondary school in inner-city Chicago had kept her wandering the world.

A combination of a need to stay away from the bitterness pervading their home after her parents' divorce and an unspoken shame at what their father had become after the accident.

A stumbling town drunk who didn't work anymore. Who spent most of his day hanging around the bar, railing against the injustice of life in spite of the fact that he had been awarded a two-hundred-thousand-dollar settlement.

Abby knew some of the payout paid their living expenses after the accident and a lot of medical bills; one of the reasons she'd pushed her father so hard to get the settlement in the first place. But Cornell had been unable to keep his job at the accounting firm he worked at. He started drinking and then he started gambling, and in the space of seven months, the money Abby had hoped would help counteract the effects of the accident was almost depleted.

That was when her mother filed for divorce. The house on the hill was sold, the assets divided between her parents. Ivy got a job working at the grocery store and moved into this apartment with Abby and her brother. Her father left town and his communications with his family became erratic.

"Elliot is very busy with his work," Abby said by way of excuse.

"As are you." Her mother's voice held an edge

that she chose to ignore. "I just hope this Bannister job doesn't take up all your time, as well."

"It won't," Abby assured her, swirling her noodles around her fork. "I don't want to spend any more time there than I have to."

Her mother's smile told her she had said exactly the right thing, but the tension permeating the atmosphere since she had told her mother about the job seemed to linger.

Then the phone rang and her mother excused herself to answer it.

Abby took another bite of food, feeling suddenly weary. She had come home to rest. To recuperate, but it seemed that wasn't going to happen here.

Please, Lord, she prayed. *Help me get through this. Help me find some peace, somewhere.*

"Please, you don't need to call," she heard her mother saying, her voice strained. Abby felt a twist of concern. Who was on the other end of the phone?

"Yes. Abby is back. She's doing a piece on the Bannisters. No. I don't like it either…" Ivy's voice faded away as she walked into her bedroom and closed the door, muffling anything else she might say.

A few moments later her mother returned, lips pressed tightly together, looking tense.

"Bad news?" Abby asked.

Her mother's gaze darted anxiously toward her, but then she shook her head slightly, as if brushing it all off. "No. No. Well…it's nothing." Ivy concentrated on her food again, but Abby knew something was up.

"I think it's something," she insisted. "Sounds like whoever called is causing you trouble."

Her mother pushed a noodle around with her fork, then eased out a heavy sigh. "That was your father. And that's not the first time he's called."

"What does he want?"

Her mother took a sip of water, smoothing a strand of hair away from her face. "He found out you were home."

"And he didn't want to talk to me?"

"I suppose I should have let him talk to you, but I didn't want to spring that on you. Not without warning."

"Was he calling about money?" Abby asked, stabbing at a meatball.

"No. He knows better than to do that," her mother said.

A couple of years after her parents' divorce, her father had called Abby asking if she could spot him a couple of hundred dollars. The only reason she gave in was that she had felt sorry for him. The next time he called her he was drunk asking for money again. This time it was only fifty. She complied. The third time he called, Abby said no. And the fourth. And the fifth.

After a while his calls became more and more sporadic.

"Whatever you do, don't you give him a single cent," Abby warned her mother.

"He didn't ask for money." Ivy sighed, rubbing her forehead with one finger. "He said he's changed. That he wants to try again. I can't. I don't have the energy. But for now, I think we should talk about something else." Her mother forced a smile. "Are you and Louisa doing anything special while you're both here?"

"Nothing special," Abby said. "This is Saddlebank, after all. But we hope to get together at the Grill and Chill for coffee sometime this week. Louisa is busy with her own visiting."

"Maybe George Bamford will be working on the premises," her mother said brightly. "He's still single."

George was the owner of the Grill and Chill. Good-looking enough, but too much scruff and grumpiness for Abby's liking.

"That's a huge no to the George situation," Abby said, needing to stop this before her mother started picking out names for her future grandchildren. "I'm not here to find a husband, Mom. Just to visit. Catch up. Decompress."

"I'm just being a mother," Ivy countered with

a melancholy smile that tugged at Abby's heart. "I want to see you settled down and happy. But you're probably right. You shouldn't put down roots in Saddlebank. This town has not been good to you."

"You're right there," Abby agreed. "But for the rest, I'm happy. I have a great job and I'm making decent money." She gave her mother a smile, though deep down she knew it for the fib it was. Truth was, she hadn't appreciated her job or the money she made for a while now. She yearned to do more photography work, less traveling. She just hadn't found a place she wanted to settle down permanently yet.

"Money that you never spend," her mother admonished gently. "You're turning thirty next month and you don't own anything more than that run-down car you're driving. You haven't had a serious relationship since high school."

Since Lee Bannister had dated her. On a bet.

"I didn't have a serious relationship then either."

And didn't that make her sound like Loser of the Decade? she thought, pushing her half-finished plate of food away.

"Which is why you should start thinking about settling down. You're not getting any younger."

"I don't know why you're pushing me to get

married," Abby said crossly. "It's not like everything turned out so great for you and Dad."

As soon as she spoke the words, she regretted her outburst.

"I'm sorry, Mom," she said. "I shouldn't have said that."

Her mother waved off her apology. "It's fine. You're right, of course. But your father and I were dealing with extenuating circumstances that caused our problems."

As Abby acknowledged her mother's comment, her foolish thoughts reverted, unwittingly, to Lee. To the moment when he'd made his little speech about putting everything behind them.

She knew she had to forgive him at some point in order to truly be free from him.

But as she looked at her mother and the reality of her situation, as she thought of a father she had once loved and now hardly heard from, she knew that forgiveness wouldn't come easy to her.

And yet, even as she formulated that thought, she couldn't stop the frisson of awareness at the time she and Lee had shared together on his ranch.

Chapter Five

Abby parked her car, then got out, hoping Lee was outside somewhere so she wouldn't have to go into the house.

But she couldn't see him anywhere on the yard, and the only sound she heard was the faint lowing of cows from somewhere on the ranch. Obviously Lee was inside, so, with a resigned sigh, she trudged up the wide cement sidewalk to the front door of the imposing house. Stained glass windows flanked the double doors, and another one arched above the entire unit framing it in a bank of light. More flowerpots with a profusion of daisies, geraniums, lobelia and some type of vine were grouped in a colorful arrangement on each side of the doorway.

Abby stopped, thankful that her ankle felt a lot better than yesterday, thankful that maybe today she would be able to walk on her own and not have to be carted around on the quad.

Behind Lee.

She pulled out a camera from her backpack and shot off a few pictures of the entrance to the house. She took more than necessary, aware she was killing time, putting off entering the Bannister home.

She looked around once more, hoping Lee would show up, but no such luck. So she sucked in a breath, whispered a prayer and pushed on the doorbell. A muffled carillon of pleasant chimes competed with the laughter she heard coming from inside.

"Come in," someone called out.

Abby stepped inside the porch, stifling a sudden attack of nerves as she closed the large wooden door behind her. Yesterday she hadn't had a chance to meet any of the other Bannisters, but now, from the noise level of the conversation drifting toward her, it sounded as though she would be seeing most of them now.

A woman of medium height, her blond hair pulled back in a ponytail emphasizing her delicate features, came to the entrance. Abby recognized her as Lee's youngest sister, Keira.

Keira's green eyes took in Abby and they briefly narrowed.

Abby understood, on one level, why Keira

might have a hard time with her. Abby was, after all, the person who had sat by her father on the other side of the conference table when their lawyers were hashing out the settlement. She was the one who had pushed Cornell to ask for as much as possible. Though Abby didn't regret the battle, she did regret the aftermath. Lee's insurance company had refused to pay, so the Bannisters ended up settling out of pocket. She knew it had caused them some financial difficulty.

But that wasn't her fault, she reminded herself.

Then Keira Bannister blinked and the coolness evaporated as she held out her hand. "Hey, Abby, good to see you," she said, giving Abby's hand a firm shake. "Come on in. We're just having an early-morning coffee."

Although Abby guessed Keira's offer was basic courtesy, she wasn't sure she wanted to face the Bannister family en masse.

But the memory of her mother living in that drab apartment made her straighten her shoulders, give Lee's sister a quick nod and follow her through the doorway. Abby knew she had nothing to apologize for.

As she followed Keira through the kitchen, Abby caught a glimpse of a large stainless-steel stove, a double fridge, granite countertops and sleek kitchen cabinets. Beyond that, tucked into a bay window, was an older wooden table with mismatched chairs pushed under it, giving the sleek, modern kitchen a homey touch. The pot of flowers sitting on the crocheted tablecloth added to the whimsy.

Then Keira turned through another doorway and Abby had to refrain from gasping.

The dining-room table alone would have filled up her mother's entire apartment. Tanner Fortier, John Argall, Heather and her parents sat around one end of the huge table that took up only one small corner of the sweeping open-beamed room. This enormous living space soared two and a half stories high. Sunlight poured in through a wall of windows flanking a large stone fireplace with its impressive chimney. Through the windows she could see the mountains cradling a portion of the basin. A massive staircase to her right swooped along one wall to the upstairs, and two heavy wooden doors led to other rooms off the main room. Antique leather furniture was grouped around a large coffee table.

A person could rope cattle in here.

"Can I get you a cup of coffee?" Keira was asking.

Abby had to drag her gaze away from the rest of the house, turning back to the gathering, all of whom were now watching her. Monty and Ellen sat at one end of the table, their smiles surprisingly welcoming. Tanner, his dark eyebrows and stubbled chin making him look like the bronc rider he was, sat beside an empty chair, one arm slung across its back. Across from him sat John Argall, apparently the new partner in the ranch, according to Burt's notes. Though she had known John all her life, his chiseled good looks could still make her catch her breath. Heather, with her long blond hair flowing over her shoulders, her stunning features and green eyes, was perfectly suited to him.

Abby couldn't help feeling slightly dowdy in her presence.

"I'll get Abby's coffee," Lee said, coming up behind her.

Abby jumped and turned toward him. Where had he come from? How many rooms were in this place?

"That is, if you want one?" He quirked a questioning eyebrow, his hands resting on his jean-clad hips. He wore a tan linen shirt that emphasized his wide shoulders, the deep brown of his hair, his tanned face.

He looked better than he should.

Abby would have preferred to simply get on with the work she had come to do, but she also knew it would be impolite to say no to the coffee, so she nodded.

"Just sit down anywhere," Lee said.

Tanner stood and pulled a chair out for her. He gave her a sly wink, as if he knew what she was feeling right now.

She murmured her thanks and walked slowly over to the table and sat down, suppressing the feeling that she was a fox in a henhouse with very large hens.

Silence, tense and heavy, fell on the gathering and then a little girl's voice called out in a panicked voice from somewhere else in the house, "Daddy, help! Please, help. Please!"

John leaped to his feet, excused himself and hurried over to the stairs. Abby guessed it was his little girl.

"Is Adana okay?" Heather called out.

John's chuckle drifted down from the upstairs region. "Yeah. She's just having trouble getting these bricks together. Apparently it's an epic disaster for her."

This was followed by general laughter, which seemed to ease the tension.

"She's kind of a drama queen, isn't she?" Tanner said to Heather. He was leaning back in his chair, one arm looped across Keira's shoulder, the other resting on the table, looking obviously at ease.

"She can be that," Heather admitted, setting her one elbow on the arm of her chair, her slender fingers touching her chin. Her gesture was unstudied, but its elegance made Abby feel suddenly gauche. "But I'm sure she'll outgrow it."

"Like *you* did?" Lee drawled, setting a mug of steaming coffee down in front of Abby. "Seems to me queen and Heather were often interchangeable words around here."

"As they should be," she retorted in true sister fashion. "I am royalty after all."

"Don't know if being crowned Rodeo Queen puts you on par with Queen Elizabeth." Lee laughed, then turned to Abby. "And how's the cut on your ankle this morning?"

"Did you hurt yourself on the ranch yesterday?" Mrs. Bannister asked, sounding concerned. "How did that happen?"

"Not yesterday and not here," Abby assured her, wondering if Ellen thought she might file a lawsuit if that was the case. "By the lookout point. I was running in my sandals…and…well, I fell and cut myself on a piece of glass." She sent a quick glance Lee's way, but his expression gave nothing away and thankfully he didn't elaborate on the embarrassing circumstances of her injury. "It's already feeling better."

"So does that mean I can take you up into the hills today?" Lee asked.

"Oh, c'mon, man," Tanner sputtered. "What kind of pickup line is that?"

"Don't pay attention to him," Keira said to Abby, elbowing Tanner in the ribs. "He's feeling feisty because he doesn't have to do any wedding stuff today."

"But I thought you had to try on your tux today," Monty interjected.

"Tux?" Tanner instantly sat up, shooting Keira a panicked look. "I thought we agreed no monkey suits." Abby tried to imagine Tanner's stubbled features and collar-length hair framed by a white shirt and black bow tie. The picture didn't gel.

"Down, boy," Keira said. "Dad's just jerking your chain. There are no tuxedos in your future."

More laughter followed this.

"Anyhow, as I was saying," Lee continued, slanting a glance her way, "I was hoping you're able to do some riding today. The forecast isn't great for tomorrow, so I thought I could take you up to the higher pasture today."

"You need to know I'm not very familiar with horses." As she uttered the words, Abby realized what a shock that might be to her present company. Each of them had probably spent more time on a horse than she had on an airplane, and considering how many frequent flyer miles she'd racked up, that was a lot of hours.

"What's to be familiar with?" Tanner asked with a lift of one broad shoulder. "Head goes in front, tail goes behind. When you sit between them, make sure you're facing the head."

"And not on the ground, facing their feet after you've been dumped in the arena like Tanner often has," John put in, entering the room, a little girl perched on his arm.

"All part of bronc riding," Tanner said with a laconic tone. "And thank goodness that's all in my past."

"Thank goodness a lot of stuff is in the past," Heather added, holding her hands out for Adana. "What was the matter, honey?"

"Bricks not work," Adana complained.

"That's okay," Heather said, taking the little girl onto her lap. "Come sit with us and I'll help you later."

Adana tucked her thumb in her mouth and dropped her curly blond head onto Heather's shoulder. Heather curled her arms around her and smiled lovingly. Ellen reached over and stroked the little girl's head, then whispered to Heather, "She looks like she could use a nap."

Monty turned to John and started talking ranch business, but while he spoke one hand rested on Keira's shoulder, sitting between him and Tanner.

Abby sipped her coffee, feeling a jolt of envy at the easy interaction between the family members. It wasn't hard to see that Monty and Ellen loved their children deeply. She suspected gatherings like this were the norm.

Again, she caught herself comparing the energy and love flowing through this room to the dull sparseness of her mother's place.

That's not Mom's fault, she reminded herself as she clutched her mug of coffee.

"You okay?" Lee asked her.

She blinked and then gave him a tight nod. "I wouldn't mind getting started..."

"Of course." He got up and turned to the others. "Abby and I are leaving now."

"I'll come with you." Monty got up as well. "Help you pick out a horse for Abby."

"I thought she could ride Tia."

"She's in foal. Which one do you think we should use, John?" Monty asked.

"Bonny is a safe bet," his partner replied.

"Never heard of her. Is she a new horse?" Lee asked.

"Not new at all," Monty put in. "We've had Bonny for about seven years, right, John? I believe you trained her."

"Then John would know, I guess."

Lee's sharp tone was a discordant note in what had otherwise been a jovial atmosphere. Seven years ago Lee was probably still in prison and Abby knew he had only been back for short visits less than a handful of times.

"He *would* know for sure," Monty said quietly. "John's been around for a while."

"And I haven't," Lee bit out, taking his mug and bringing it to the sink.

Abby glanced from Monty to Lee, who was stalking toward the porch, and then quickly got up to follow. "Thanks for the coffee," she said to Ellen even though Lee had been the one to bring it to her.

"Will we see you later for lunch?" Ellen asked curiously.

"Um, not sure." Abby had no idea if she was expected to be part of the social network of the ranch. Part of her hoped not. But another small part of her felt a yearning for the closeness of this family.

She picked up her backpack and followed Monty out the door. Lee was already outside. Monty held the door open and Abby gave him a quick smile of thanks.

A few clouds had slipped across the sun while they were inside and Abby zipped up her hoodie, hoping she was dressed warm enough for riding up in the hills.

"I, uh, only have running shoes." She looked down at the bright pink sneakers she had put on this morning. "I hope that's okay."

"They'll work good enough for what you're doing," Monty said, dropping his worn cowboy hat on his head. Lee was well ahead of them. Abby wanted to hurry but didn't want to hurt herself again, so she walked at a slower pace.

"I hope you don't mind my asking," Monty continued, "but how are your parents doing? I see your mother from time to time at the grocery store and I say hello, but that's about it. I haven't seen your father around. I do think of them and pray for them."

Abby shot him a quick look, touched by his concern and the fact that he thought to remember them in his prayers.

"I don't mind you asking," she answered. "My dad has his struggles. I haven't heard from him for a while, though he did contact me a couple of months ago. My mom is doing okay. Her job keeps her busy and she's managing."

"I know this might not be the time or place," Monty said, looking ahead as they walked. "But I haven't had an opportunity to speak to you face-to-face since the settlement, and I want you to know that Lee lives with a lot of regrets over what happened. What you saw a moment ago is the result of those regrets."

Abby's heart twisted, her own thoughts a sudden turmoil. She understood what Monty was doing. A father speaking on behalf of his son, but at the same time, she knew that regrets wouldn't change what had happened to her family.

"You may as well know, I didn't want to take this job on," she confided. "But I decided to accept it because part of me wants to put this mess of my father's accident—and Lee's role in it—behind me. I want to be done with it all."

"I'm glad to hear that," Monty said gruffly. "He's a good son. He's lost a lot in all of this too."

Abby heard what he was saying, but nonetheless, as she looked around the ranch, as she thought of the grandiose house she had just left, the legacy Lee could take on if he just said yes, it was hard not to compare it to what she had personally lost.

Somehow, in spite of it all, Lee had still come out ahead.

"You're sure you're okay with this?" Lee adjusted Abby's stirrup and looked up at her, silhouetted against the cloudy sky, sitting on Bonny's back. The sun slipped from behind a cloud and burnished her reddish hair, creating a halo effect, putting her face in shadows. He felt an unwelcome stirring in his chest. The hesitant beginnings of attraction.

They're more than beginnings. You were attracted to her before.

"It's high up here" was all she said.

Lee couldn't fathom her tension around Bonny. Even though he had been away from horses for a number of years, once he stepped out into the corrals and saw them come running at his call, he felt a sense of belonging. He moved easily among them, singling out the ones he would be using. As he had bridled and saddled, his hands found the rhythm, working with the horses, buckling, tightening, assuring. It felt so natural to be around them, he couldn't imagine feeling as uncomfortable as Abby looked.

"We could use the quad." He felt he had to offer, but he sincerely hoped she wouldn't take him up on it. For one thing, the quad wasn't as nimble as the horses and would be more awkward to get over some of the rockier places in the trail. For another, he wasn't sure he wanted her sitting right behind him again as she had done yesterday. He had been far too aware of her and wasn't keen on experiencing that again. Because, like it or not, he and Abby were an impossible and complicated combination.

Lee gritted his teeth, knowing he had no one to blame but himself. He'd had his chance with her, and his own poor choices had messed that up.

Besides, he was probably leaving again once his sister was married.

"No. That's fine," she said, cutting into his thoughts. "I want to try this. After all, if I'm expected to come on the cattle drive, then I better get some horse time in."

"Good point. Now stand up in the stirrups so I can check the length," he instructed, hoping the initial preparations would ease her skittishness. "If this saddle works, I'll make sure to keep it adjusted for you."

"No one else needs it?" she asked as she slowly stood. She wobbled, then sat down again.

"No. We have plenty of saddles. One of the benefits of having a saddle maker in the family. Ankle okay?" he asked before he slid the casing down over the buckle. She had enough clearance from the saddle and the stirrups were okay.

"It's not my ankle that's the problem," she said, her nervousness seeming to grow. "But I'll be okay as long as my horse behaves."

"If my dad vouches for Bonny, you can be sure she's bombproof. He wouldn't put you on a horse that would cause you any trouble." As if to prove a point, he ran his hands down Bonny's withers and the horse didn't even flinch.

His father had offered to help get the horses

saddled up and Lee recognized the gesture for what it was. A small peace offering for the quarrel they'd had in the house. Lee knew he shouldn't have been so short with his dad, but every time he saw Monty and John talking together, he felt shut out. He knew they didn't do it intentionally; it was the reality of his situation. He was the one who had stayed away, the son who hadn't claimed his inheritance even though he had his reasons.

"Bombproof sounds good," Abby said, still sounding skittish.

"If you want, I can take your knapsack with me," Lee offered, waiting beside her to make sure she was comfortable.

Bonny shifted, snorted, then shook her head, her bridle clanking, and Abby jumped again. But then she relaxed slightly. "No, thanks. I always carry my own equipment." Today she had also taken a tripod, which she had slipped through a sleeve across the back of her knapsack.

"If you're sure, we can get going." Lee patted Bonny on the side, as if to remind her of his expectations, then walked over to Bandit and in one easy motion mounted the horse.

He grinned at the familiar feel of the saddle, his feet in the stirrups, the reins in his hand. His father had made this saddle, but Lee hadn't used it for over four years. The last time he was back at the ranch, it had been winter and too cold to go riding. The time before that it was only a short visit.

This was the longest stretch of time he would be back at the ranch since he'd left.

He turned Bandit away from the hitching post, nudged him gently in the side, signaling a walk, then led the way toward the gates of the first pastures. His heart lifted at the thought of the ride ahead.

"We'll be going across this pasture to the fence on the far side," he said, turning back to Abby, "Through another set of gates and then through the trees, leading to the upper pasture."

She gave him a quick nod, but he could see from the way her lips were pressed together that she was still feeling tense. At least she wasn't hauling on the reins like many first-time riders, treating them like brakes, holding the horse's head down and confusing him.

Well, she said she was willing, so she would figure it out, he thought, reaching down and unlatching the gate from the back of his horse. He rode through, Bandit pushing the gate open with his body, then waited for Abby to follow.

"That's a neat trick," she said, sounding a little less nervous.

"Sheer laziness," he returned. "Don't feel like

getting off and on the horse." He latched the gate and then continued on. He kept his horse alongside Abby's, checking as the horses walked over the pasture.

She released a slow breath as the horses ambled along. "Well, this isn't half as scary as I imagined," she said. "When you mentioned riding, I pictured us galloping across the open fields, me screaming and clinging for dear life to the saddle. Not an elegant thought."

He laughed. "This is a ride, not a rodeo."

She smiled and he could see her slowly settling into the saddle, releasing the tension that held her in its grip. "I think I can get used to this." She patted Bonny on the side, letting the horse know she was okay.

Lee rested one hand on his thigh, the other holding the reins loosely, moving with the horse. The scent of warm grass, leather and horseflesh wafted around him, filling in an emptiness in his life that, till now, nothing else had been able to replenish. He looked around at the hills as familiar to him as the lines of his own hands, the mountains he had watched through nineteen seasons of his life. He knew what kept him away, but at the same time, he felt an unspoken yearning slowly ease away.

"You look happy," Abby said.

Lee looked back at her, somewhat dismayed

to catch her studying him. At least she didn't have that camera out again.

"Content is more like it," he returned.

"Same thing, isn't it?"

He shook his head. "Not at all. Contentment has a depth to it that can't be as easily flipped on and off as happiness. I've discovered that happiness is too fickle an emotion."

"That's…profound."

"Stick around, girl," he said. "I'm just getting started."

"A veritable font of wisdom."

His lips twisted ruefully. "I learned a few things in prison."

And, as often happened when he used the *P* word, an awkward silence fell between them.

Thankfully they had come to the next gate. Lee opened it, let her through and when he closed it, he looked up to see her, camera in hand, lifting it up to take a picture.

He held up his hand. "Please. Don't."

"Will Bonny be okay with me doing this?"

"Bonny's fine. Loop the reins around your arm so you don't lose them, though. As for the camera, I just don't want you taking my picture."

"I'm not taking your picture," she murmured, clicking away, one-handed, even though Lee could see that the lens was pointed at him. "I am capturing a man, a horse and a legacy."

"Then you should be taking pictures of my dad. After all, it's his ranch and his legacy." He didn't like the faintly defensive tone that crept into his voice. His father had been making his disappointment with Lee known all through high school. Mowing down and seriously injuring Abby's father had simply been the final straw in Monty's estimation of Lee's life and his prospects. Spending three years in prison, and seeing people's reactions to that episode in his life, had created a deep humility in Lee along with the realization that nothing was owed to him. All he had was simply through God's grace.

Lee clucked to his horse and walked in front of her, leading the way. The path, well trodden by the cows, was wide enough for two horses to ride abreast, but Abby seemed content to stay behind. And, truth to tell, he preferred it. Something about her piercing gaze unsettled him. Every now and again he heard the whirr and click of her camera, but this time he kept his comments to himself.

After half an hour of riding, the trees broke open into a sweeping, open basin. He stopped at the top of it, looking down the gentle slope to where the cows were grazing below him, brown and block dots scattered over the lush green hills. Farther in the distance, he saw the silver thread of the creek cutting through the pasture, tumbling down toward the far pastures of the ranch.

"Are these all your cattle?"

"This bunch is only part of them," he said as he dismounted, his saddle creaking gently. Abby hadn't ridden before, so he thought she might appreciate the break. "Dad keeps the cattle scattered over three different pastures." Lee walked over to assist Abby, but she was already carefully getting off the mare. He stood close enough to help if she needed it, but not so close that she would feel he was hovering.

"So these are only a third of the herd?" Abby asked, letting her backpack slip off her arm and lowering it to the grass once she was all the way down, still holding the reins in the other hand.

"These are the first-calf heifers. They represent a quarter of the herd. The older cows with calves at foot are in another pasture. Those are the ones we'll be moving for the anniversary celebrations." He held out his hand to her. "Give me Bonny's reins. Then you can take pictures easier."

As she handed them over, their hands brushed and Lee had to fight the urge to tighten his fingers around her hand.

Abby, seemingly unaffected by the moment, walked slowly to the edge of the basin, knelt down and started shooting. Then she checked her camera, made a few adjustments and took a few more shots.

While she worked, Lee drew in a long, slow breath. A smile curved his lips as he looked back toward the cattle grazing along the vast open spaces. The sight wrapped around his soul and curled around it close like a fist.

Ever since the accident, he had felt disoriented and off-kilter, as if his world was always tilted. But now he felt as though he had found solid ground. A firm foundation on the Bannister legacy, unbroken and unchanging for one hundred and fifty years.

Until now.

Your father doesn't have to be the last Bannister on this land. You could stay.

But behind that tantalizing thought came the reality of his own history and the shame he had brought on the family by his irresponsible actions. Could he truly let go of that? Did he dare to think he could simply make a decision to come back and there would be room for him? What's more, did he have the courage to face a tight-knit community affected by his actions?

"You said it was your great-great-grandparents who settled this place," Abby said as she walked back to where her backpack lay, her voice penetrating his thoughts. "But how did they get started? How did they survive?"

"*Barely* survived, that is," Lee replied, sparing her a quick look. "They had some horrific years after they first arrived. There weren't many neighbors to help out, and times were lean, according to the stories handed down. I think Great-grandpa headed down to Virginia City to work the gold mines a few years. He made some cash, which helped them get through some of the tough years. It also helped them expand as they slowly got their feet under them."

He paused for a moment, looking out once again over the gently rolling hills, before continuing. "They made it through the Indian wars, had a couple of sons who worked alongside them on the ranch and then those boys went on to work on the railroad when it came through." Turning toward Abby, he fixed his gaze squarely on hers. Her look of rapt fascination prompted him to go on. "In the great blizzard of the 1880s, I think they lost half the herd. But they stayed, expanded, worked together, married, had their own boys who took over from them… And so it went, the ranch getting passed down through the generations."

"Has it stayed intact all through the years?"

"It's been fluid, depending on who stayed and

who left. At one time the ranch was larger, but it got split off a few generations ago. My dad's second cousin, Keith McCauley, still ranches here, but who knows what will happen to his place?"

"How come?" she asked curiously.

"Well, he only had the three girls and they haven't shown the least bit of interest in his place. My grandfather ranched with Keith's brother but bought him out when he wanted to leave the valley. Keith still owns a fair-sized ranch, though."

Lee stopped there, thinking back over the history of the ranch that his father would, from time to time, expound on. "I have to confess, I never paid a lot of attention to the whole history of the place when my parents were telling me. My mind was always somewhere else, thinking of all the places I'd sooner be than spending the rest of my life living in the basin and chasing cows."

"And now?" Abby's question underlined his own shifting state of mind.

"I don't know." His response came out reluctantly, but truthfully.

"You like the work that you're doing now?"

Lee didn't answer right away, thinking of the long, hard days he put in at his job as a driller in the oil patch. The boring evenings staying in camps watching television, playing cards. Going to bed and doing it all over again the next day.

"It's work" was all he said.

Abby took a few more pictures, then pulled out a notebook.

"I understand your father runs Angus cows?" she asked, jotting some notes in her book.

Lee gladly switched to a safer topic of conversation. "Dad made the switch to black and red Angus cows when he took over the ranch from his father, against Grandpa Lee's protests. It was a smart move. Angus calves are thrifty and the cows are great mothers. They're not as large at weaning as your Simmentals or Charolais, but much easier to handle."

"You sound as though you speak from experience."

Lee nodded and rolled up the sleeve of his shirt, exposing a long scar that ran down his forearm. "Got this when we were trying to load the last of the Charolais Grandpa Lee was so crazy about. We couldn't get them on the truck and then, all of a sudden, one turned and ran straight at me. I had to jump the fence but got my arm caught up on a nail." He winced at the memory. "So, suffice it to say, me and my sisters weren't sad to see the last of them heading down the road."

"Did you and your sisters help out a lot on the ranch?" Abby asked, looking up from her notebook.

"Though we always had a hired hand or two, helping was part and parcel of being a Bannister. Even Heather, who came to live here when she was ten, was expected to pitch in. She would yammer and complain, but when it was calving season, or time for shots or time to move cows, we all had to saddle up and cowboy up." He let a smile spread across his lips as his mind slipped back to those times. "Mind you, I wasn't always the most willing participant when I was older. I much preferred spending my time whooping it up with my friends."

"Mitch and David?" Abby asked, her voice quiet as if she was hesitant to mention the names of the orangutans he hung out with.

"Yeah. Those two." He shook his head, remembering, with some shame, his times with his so-called friends. They had been with him at the party that sent his and Abby's father's lives into a downward spiral.

"Well, those two were nothing but trouble in high school. Not the nicest guys."

"And their behavior just grew worse after high school," Lee murmured.

"What do you mean?" Abby asked, furrowing her brow.

Lee's horse whickered lightly; Bonny bobbed her head as if in reply. Lee fought the urge to move the horses on, as if to leave the past—and his no-good friends—at this place.

"Those aren't my secrets to tell," he said curtly, thinking of the physical and mental abuse Mitch, Heather's ex-husband, had heaped on Heather while they were married. David, as well, had his dark history. At a party that had gotten out of control, he had forced himself on Keira. The backlash of those actions had reverberated through Keira's life and had almost cost her her relationship with Tanner, David's brother.

"But you look angry." She narrowed her eyes at him. "Why is that?

Turning away, he ran the ends of the horse's reins through one hand, thinking what to say and how much to tell Abby. She was a reporter, after all.

"All I'll say is both those guys created huge trauma for my sisters." His mouth hardened into a tight line and then he sighed. "I struggle with thinking I could have prevented that as well if I had quit hanging around with them like my parents always pleaded with me to do. And I shudder to think what I would have turned out like had I stuck around here in Saddlebank."

Silence followed that admission.

"Then maybe it's a good thing you ended up in jail."

Lee swung his gaze back to Abby, but she wasn't joking. Her expression was dead serious.

And as her words settled between them, he wondered if maybe she wasn't right.

Chapter Six

Abby restrained a gasp, wondering how she dared to speak those words aloud.

And from Lee's inscrutable expression, she wished she could take them back.

"I'm sorry," she said, but even as she spoke, she felt as if her apology undermined her own father's pain.

Lee held up one hand as if to stop her. "No. You had every right to speak your mind." He gave her a half smile. "I deserved what happened to me, but it helped me turn my life around. I started attending the church services and the pastor helped me with my faith journey. I guess I was in a place where I had no choice but to listen, so I finally did."

"Well, that's good, I guess" was all she could say.

"I know it wasn't a good thing for you and

your family, but it made a difference for me, so it's a mixed bag." He looked away from her again and Abby's reaction shifted and tangled. Pictures of her father, memories of the fights her parents had all melded, fueling the resentment she always felt whenever she thought of Lee. "I can't change what happened," he continued, "but there isn't a day that I don't regret what I did. That I wish I could fix it somehow."

It was the sincerity in his voice that caught her attention.

Away from Lee she could make him out to be whatever monster she wanted him to be. But hearing what he said about her father, hearing the regrets he carried, banked the anger that had powered her emotions since the accident.

She knew she should forgive him, but she still struggled with a sense that she was betraying her family.

But the weariness clinging to her the past few years whispered at her to let go. Keeping the fires of injustice against her family stoked and burning took a lot of energy. Maybe forgiving him was what she needed to do for her own peace of mind. She had hoped to find some type of closure by doing this piece. Could this be the first step?

"Forgive as I have forgiven you."

The remnant of a Bible passage flittered into

her mind, and she let it settle. It couldn't hurt to consider forgiving him. Her own life wasn't perfect and Lee seemed to be wrestling with his own regrets. He hadn't come out of this unscathed in spite of his family's money.

Is that what matters? That the scales are balanced? That you find out that he suffered, as well?

"I appreciate what you said," she finally replied. "It's been hard, but like you said at the beginning of my visit, we need to find a way to move on. You've given me lots to think about."

"That's all I can ask for," he said gruffly.

She had planned to simply acknowledge his comment, then look away.

But when his dark eyes locked on hers, she saw pain in their depths.

Her heart twisted with sympathy for him, and feelings from a simpler time in their lives were resurrected. For the space of a few, heavy heartbeats, he was the young man she had had such a crazy crush on. The strappingly handsome man who had danced with her at the prom, had held her close. Had told her she was beautiful. The first man who had made her feel breathless with just one look.

That same breath now slowed and she felt her hand rise, as if to comfort him. Just in time she caught herself and dragged her gaze away from his, feeling as if she were coming up for air.

She felt suddenly off balance.

Silly, foolish romantic, she chastised herself, frustrated that all it took was a soulful look from those deep brown eyes and she was back in high school. *You can't let that girlish crush influence your decisions*.

"Glad that's out of the way," she said, struggling to find some levity. "Onward and upward." She slipped the camera back in her bag. "Where to next, cowboy?"

Lee looked at her as if surprised at her response. Then he handed her Bonny's reins. "I thought we could go a bit farther to the back pasture. You can get a better view."

"Of the extensive Bannister estate?" she said with a wry tone.

"Of the ranch," he said, a glower showing her that he didn't fully appreciate her comment.

She knew she was being flippant, but it was the only defense she had against him.

And the way he was making her feel, she knew she would need everything she could use to keep him at arm's length.

Lifting her chin, Abby slipped her knapsack over her shoulders, looped Bonny's reins around her hand, then carefully mounted her. The cut on her ankle didn't bother her as much, but she still preferred to err on the side of caution. Once she was up in the saddle, Lee clucked to his horse and with a nudge got him walking along the edge of the basin.

Abby couldn't help a glimmer of admiration as Lee rode away from her. His movements easily matched Bandit's, his hands light on the reins, his hips moving in sync with his horse's walk. The angle of the sun highlighted horse and rider, now silhouetted against the mountains beyond the basin, and she had to stop herself from pulling out her camera and taking a picture.

She had enough photos of Lee, and if she took any more, she was venturing too far into the same place that had gotten her into trouble when she was taking photos of Lee for the yearbook and Mitch and David had found out.

She pushed that thought down, focusing instead on the land around her, looking for camera angles, light and shadows.

After twenty minutes of riding, they turned a corner and were looking over another cow-dotted pasture. A fence line snaked down the side of the hill toward the creek spooling out well below them.

"Did you want some pictures?" he asked, stopping.

"I'd love to get some of those calves," Abby

said, pointing to a group of calves, tails up, racing across the pasture like a group of teenagers without curfew.

Lee nodded then dismounted with an easy movement. Abby knew she wouldn't be able to get off as smoothly. She could feel the muscles in her leg starting to hurt and her ankle was getting sore.

Obviously Lee had noticed her discomfort as well and headed over, leading Bandit.

"You okay?" he asked as he tied his horse to the tree.

"Just a bit stiff."

"We can go home after this."

"Yeah. Might be a good idea," she admitted, feeling foolish. Lee was probably just getting warmed up. He certainly didn't look as though the hour ride was causing him any pain.

Abby set up her tripod, deciding to try some telephoto shots this time. She changed lenses, then took out her notebook and scribbled down some of the things Lee had told her before they left her scattered brain.

"So, what's easier for you, the picture taking or the writing?" he asked curiously.

"Pictures. For sure," she returned.

"Well, they say a picture is worth a thousand words."

"Yeah, but they take up a thousand times the

memory on my computer," she returned as she put her notebook back in her knapsack. "Especially once I start editing them."

"Do you do a lot of photo editing?"

She was pleasantly surprised at his interest. "Depends on the picture," she said, giving him a quick look before leaning forward to look through her lens. "Sometimes, if I've used a filter on the camera, not as much. But mostly I spend about twenty minutes or so per photo enhancing the light, tweaking the contrast, bumping up the color, sometimes adding some blur. Again, depends on what effect I'm trying to achieve."

"And the writing part. Will you be showing my father what you do before it goes to your editor?"

Abby shook her head as she adjusted the tripod. "I don't think so. I'm writing the piece from my point of view, and if I know that your father or someone else attached to the ranch could have input, it won't be a true piece."

"Truth can be twisted around depending on your point of view," Lee said.

Was she being overly sensitive or had his tone sounded as sharp as she thought?

Don't overreact. Ask questions first.

Maddie's advice filtered into her mind just as Abby was about to protest. "What do you mean by that?" she asked.

He frowned at her, then shook his head. "Nothing. Just…thinking out loud."

"I get the feeling there is more to it than that," she countered. "Is this connected to what happened here in Saddlebank? After the accident?"

For some reason she wasn't ready to analyze why she wanted to understand his side of the story. *It's just what a good journalist does*, she reminded herself.

"The media outlets that covered the whole event, both local and statewide, made me out to be some kind of spoiled rich kid whose parents let him run wild without supervision. It made for better press than simply a story of some kid making a horrible mistake." Jaw tightening, Lee squatted down, squinting at the view below them. "My parents were good people who did the right thing. All the mistakes were mine. The choices were mine and the consequences were mine."

He stopped himself there and gave his head a shake, as if to stop any further revelations, then glanced up at her. "Sorry. I suppose I don't appreciate what my parents had to deal with either."

Abby held his steady gaze, letting his words settle into her own thoughts. She knew she was guilty of the same conclusion, and hearing him give voice to her own perceptions made her feel contrite, as well.

"I'm not going to editorialize, if that helps," she said. "I'm simply writing a piece about the ranch. You and your family can see the final draft when it's done, but it's only about the legacy of this ranch. Nothing more."

Abby sensed he was still unsure, but he simply gave her a curt nod. Abby felt annoyed, wondering what right he had to mistrust her. If anyone had grounds to feel that way, it was her.

Not him.

She looked through the camera again, rotating it around, then aimed it toward the pasture. A group of calves raced past again, but as they did, something else caught her attention and she zoomed in, focusing. A calf stood by itself, looking toward a clump of bushes.

Puzzled, Abby turned her camera, then saw what the calf was looking at. A cow, lying on its side. It wasn't moving.

"I think there's something wrong with that cow," she murmured, looking up at Lee. "You should have a look."

Lee glanced at her, took his Stetson off, then bent over, looking through the camera's viewfinder. He straightened, looked over the camera, then through it again.

Then he strode over to his horse.

"What's wrong?" Abby asked as Lee untied him.

"That cow is dead," Lee said. "I'll have to rescue that calf."

Abby grabbed her knapsack. "I'm coming with you."

"Just stay here," Lee warned.

But Abby knew this would add some drama to the piece. She left her other camera on the tripod, snatched another one out of the backpack, looped it around her neck.

All stiffness forgotten, she clambered into the saddle and followed Lee down the hill toward where the calf still stood.

Lee glanced back, frustrated that Abby had followed him down here. Calves born out on pasture tended to be more skittish. The more people around, the more flighty this one would be. He held up his hand as they got closer, signaling to Abby to stay back. He stopped Bandit and slowly dismounted, but as he came nearer, he could see the calf was swaying on its feet, its sides hollow. It gave another weak bleat toward its mother and then, as Lee slowly approached it, it wobbled and lay down.

Lee slipped his fingers inside its mouth. Instead of a good hard suck with its rough tongue, the calf swiped feebly at his fingers. Its mouth was cool, which meant the calf had probably not drunk yet.

A quick look at the cow showed him it was, indeed, dead. The afterbirth was already dry. Who knew how long ago this calf had been born? It had probably not even had its first drink yet. Lee bent over, fitted his arms under the calf's front and back legs, then slowly stood up. He turned to see Abby off her horse, snapping pictures of him. Again.

He couldn't be bothered to be annoyed.

"Can you help me?" he called out. "I need to get this calf back to the ranch."

"Is the mother really dead?"

"Yes." He didn't mean to sound brusque, but he was feeling the pressure of time running out. If they didn't get some warm milk or, hopefully, colostrum into this calf, it would die.

Abby was off her horse and walking toward him. "What can I do?"

"I'll need some help getting this calf up on my horse. Push up on the back end while I try to lift up the front."

She seemed to figure out what he wanted, and in a surprising few minutes, Lee had the calf draped over the front of his saddle.

"Hold Bandit's reins while I get on," he directed.

Again, Abby was quick to respond and a few

seconds later, Lee was up on the saddle, the calf lying across his lap.

"I'm heading back to the ranch," he said. "Can you catch up?"

Abby nodded, then hurried back to Bonny and quickly got on. Lee kept Bandit to a slow trot, hoping the calf wouldn't get too jostled. They passed the spot where Abby still had her other camera up on the tripod. He glanced back as he passed it. Abby was already out of the saddle and quickly packing up.

"If you don't see me, don't worry," he called out. "Bonny will find her way back to the ranch. Just trust her lead."

Abby nodded again, as she made quick work of collapsing her tripod. Lee looked ahead, feeling guilty for leaving her behind, but right now his priority was this calf.

"Just stay alive, little guy," he said, holding it steady with one hand while he managed the reins with the other. The calf's hair was sticking up in stiff spikes, showing Lee that the mother hadn't even licked it off after it was born.

His concern grew when he heard the calf's labored breathing. He slowed down a couple of times, but then the state of the calf would urge him on.

He glanced back, but he couldn't see Abby. Once again, he was torn between concern for the calf and concern for Abby. He knew Bonny would find her way home, but it was hard not to worry. Then the sound of hooves behind him made him turn in time to see Bonny trotting his way, Abby bobbing awkwardly up and down on his back. Poor girl had no style, but she seemed to have lots of grit. She was hanging on to the pommel of the saddle with one hand, her backpack bouncing behind her.

In spite of the circumstances, the grim look on her pretty face made him smile. He was fairly sure she would be mighty sore tomorrow.

Finally the trees broke open and he could see the ranch in the distance. The gate was ahead and he made quick work of opening it.

"Can you close the gates behind you?" he called out as he rode through it.

All he heard was a faint yes and that was enough for him. He stepped up the pace, still supporting the calf, who now had its eyes closed, as if it had given up.

He got through the second gate, then rode Bandit to the barn, dismounted, made quick work of tying his horse up and brought the newborn calf into the barn. A quick glance around the yard showed him that both his father and John were gone. He was on his own.

Calving pens lined the walls of the barn on both sides, and Lee brought the calf into the first pen, closest to the door. In spite of the warmth outside, it was cool and dark in here and, unfortunately, there was no straw in the pen.

"Sorry, little guy," he crooned, laying the calf down on the pitted wooden floor. "I'll fix this up in a minute." He ran out of the pen and down the dirt-packed alley to the back of the barn. He heard panting and looked down to see Sugar, trotting alongside him, appearing curious.

"Got a sick calf," he said to the dog as he grabbed a straw bale from a stack at the back of the barn. He heaved it up by the strings and carried it, one-handed, back to the pen. Sugar, hot on his heels, followed him inside. Lee didn't think the calf would even notice, so he just left the dog be.

Lee busted out the bale, sprinkled it around, nested it around the calf and then rushed out the door.

Almost running smack into Abby.

"What else do you need to do?" she asked breathlessly. "How can I help?"

"We need to get some colostrum into that calf as soon as possible. Can you sit with him and hold his head up? I'll be back in a few minutes. The calf is in the first pen to your left, just inside the door."

Then he hurried away, racing to the room off the barn. Sugar looked from him to Abby as if unsure of who to follow but then, for some reason, turned and trotted back into the barn.

Lee yanked open the cupboard doors above the sink. Thankfully everything was all in the same place. Plastic bags of colostrum powder on one side neatly stacked. Bottles and tubes on the other all clean and ready to go. A few minutes later, he was hurrying to the barn with a warm pail of the colostrum and the other supplies tucked under his arm.

Please, Lord, don't let that calf be dead, he prayed as he scooted into the barn.

He heard a rustle of straw as he burst into the pen. Abby sat on the floor, the calf's head on her lap. Sugar was sitting in the doorway, head cocked to one side, watching Abby stroking the calf's side, singing softly. She looked up when Lee came in and he saw a flush darken her cheeks, making the faint sprinkling of freckles across her nose stand out even more.

He stopped and stared. She looked beautiful, sitting there, the light from the window behind her slanting across her face, illuminating her hair.

Then he shook his reaction off.

"We need to get this into him right away," he said, turning his attention back to the calf. "Can you hold this steady?"

She nodded, taking the large plastic bottle

from him. He carefully poured in some of the milk, took the bottle from her and screwed on the oversize nipple.

"Okay, we need to get him up on his haunches," he instructed.

She didn't balk at picking up the calf and followed his orders, shifting the calf so it was perched on its back legs, front ones straight down in front of him. Lee opened its mouth with his finger and quickly slid the nipple inside. It immediately popped to the other side of its mouth. The calf had barely the strength to suck.

"I think he's too weak," he muttered, running his finger along the outside of the calf's throat, trying to encourage him to start swallowing, which would stimulate the sucking reflex.

After ten minutes of frustration, Lee could see they weren't getting anywhere and the calf was slowly going down. They were running out of time.

"Now what?" Abby whispered, stroking the calf's sides.

Lee could see she was genuinely distressed and he gave her a reassuring smile. "Now we try tube-feeding it. You'll need to lay him down to help me with this." He set the bottle down and got the bag and tube ready. "I hope you're okay with this."

"I'll do what needs to be done," Abby declared. She looked grim, but she seemed game.

"Good girl," he said, clipping the tube and opening up the heavy plastic bag attached to it. "Pour the rest of the milk in here." Once it was filled, he sealed it off, then rinsed off the long, hard stick attached to the tube. "Can you hold this while I get him up again?"

Abby took the bag and tube as Lee straddled the calf, got him up.

"For now, just hold up the bag," he said to her. "And hand me the tube attached to it."

"What are you doing?" she asked as he opened the calf's mouth and slowly eased the solid portion of the tube down.

"The calf is too weak to suck, so the only way we're going to get any kind of nutrition into him is to get a tube directly into his stomach and give him the milk that way."

Abby grimaced but continued holding the bag as Lee gently inserted the tube. He blew out his breath, listening to the calf. It was breathing properly, so all was well. "Now undo the clip—slowly," he told Abby.

Minutes later the bag was empty and Lee gently removed the tube. He laid the calf down and stroked its head. "Way to go, little guy," he murmured, easing out a relieved sigh.

"So, what do we do now?"

"Wait." Then he stood up. "And for now, I need to tend to the horses."

"I'll stay here," Abby said, looking down at the calf, her hand on its side. "Keep an eye on him."

"You don't mind?"

"Not at all. I feel invested in the adventure now, and it will give me some fantastic material for my story. Lee Bannister, rescuer of the weak and helpless."

He shot her a bemused look as he gathered up the supplies, wondering if she was being sarcastic, but her expression was serious. "I'm just glad you saw him. You had as much to do with this rescue as I did."

"This little adventure was an eye-opener," she admitted. "In more ways than one."

Lee held her steady gaze, hearing a subtext to her words. "If you're referring to what I said about my regrets, you need to know I was sincere."

"I got that."

Her pretty amber eyes were still locked on him and he couldn't look away. Nor did he want to. Old emotions and attractions, simmering beneath the surface ever since he saw her again, rose, sifting into the moment.

"I wish things were different for us," he said thickly, the words spilling out before he could filter them.

Her eyes widened, her lips parted and he heard a faint intake of her breath. Then she tore her gaze away, looking down at the calf, who was now asleep.

He turned to leave. He shouldn't have put that on her, but just as he closed the door of the pen behind him, he thought he heard a faintly whispered "Me too."

Chapter Seven

Abby squeezed her lips together, her heart pounding in her chest. She hoped, yes, even prayed, that Lee hadn't heard her whispered confession.

What had made her say that? Her own regrets at how things had turned out between them? But what did she have to regret and why was she still mulling that over all these years later?

Abby stroked the calf, looking down at the poor, bedraggled creature. Seeing Lee working with him was shocking on one level and yet, at the same time, she saw a man deeply concerned with the life of this helpless creature.

And that, in itself, was creating a quieting in her soul and opening up the doors she thought she had firmly shut on her memories of Lee.

Silly girl, she thought. *Still can't outgrow that high school crush.*

On the other hand, she knew it was something more than a crush. Abby had never been the kind of girl who dated unintentionally. She had promised herself, as a young woman, that if she went out with someone, it would be with serious intent. Since high school she'd only dated one other man, and she was the one who ended that relationship because she was gone so much.

"Kind of a sad situation, isn't it?" she cooed to the calf, stroking it once more. Since they had fed it the poor creature hadn't moved. Abby wondered, with a start, if it was even still alive. She heard a whine and gave the dog, sitting in the opening of the pen, a self-conscious smile. "Yes, I talk to animals," she said.

Sugar seemed to see that as an invitation and came to join her, dropping down with a sigh beside her, laying her head on her paws.

Abby spared the dog a quick pet and was rewarded with a wet lick of her hand.

Then Lee was back, pushing open the wooden door to the pen with a creak. And Abby's foolish heart started thumping again. She wasn't going to look up, but she couldn't help a quick glance his way, only to find him looking at her, his expression serious.

"Is he still alive?" he asked, crouching down on the opposite side of the calf.

"He's still warm, though barely moving." She stroked it again, as if willing the animal to live.

"Sugar, back," he said to the dog.

The canine looked up, glancing at Abby as if hoping she would intervene. But she didn't think she should, so Sugar got up and trotted to the doorway.

"I don't want her disturbing the calf," Lee explained. He moved to the calf's head and slipped his fingers in its mouth. Then he smiled. "Its mouth is warmer than before, so its blood is circulating and warming it up. So far so good."

"When do you have to feed it again?" she asked, getting up to get her camera as he washed his hands in the other pail of water he had taken along. She wanted to document this part of the rescue operation.

Lee dried his hands and then pulled his phone out of his pocket, glancing at the screen. "I think I'll try again in about four hours." He gave her a contrite smile. "Sorry for cutting the ride short."

"No…please don't apologize," she said, waving his comment off. "Of course you had to take care of this calf." Releasing a pent-up breath, she took the lens cap off her camera and turned her attention back to her work. She sat down, framing the calf, looking for the right light. Sunlight slanted into the pen, illuminating the dust motes and casting interesting shadows. She shot off a couple of pictures before looking back at Lee. "Do you have to do this more often? Rescue orphan calves?"

"Since Dad switched to Angus cows and calves on pasture, not nearly as often. When we ran Simmentals and calved in March, I can't count how often we'd bring a calf and her mother back to these pens." He grimaced. "We'd have calves born in a spring snowstorm, mothers calving in a puddle of water, calves we had to pull and then doctor up like this. It kept us way too busy and was tough on the babies."

"Not hard to see you know what you're doing," she said, shifting her position and snapping a few more photos. "And that you care about the animals. A real cattleman."

"I don't know about that," he muttered. "Like I mentioned earlier, when I was young, I could hardly wait to get away from here. I thought working on the ranch, living in Saddlebank, was the most boring thing in the world."

"Is that why you hung out with Mitch and David?"

"Probably," he admitted. "Life was exciting around those two. Trouble was, it was the wrong kind of excitement."

"And now David's dead and Mitch is being charged with fraud." Again, the words came out before she could stop them. Why couldn't she just leave this be?

"I guess what goes around comes around," Lee said. "My dad always warned me about them. Told me they were bad news. That they loved nothing more than disturbing the status quo, and letting people know exactly what they thought of them…"

"I know that from personal experience," she murmured, checking through the pictures she had just taken.

"What do you mean?"

Abby bit her lip, mentally kicking herself as she scrolled through the photos, most of her attention on Lee's question. Could she not learn to keep her mouth shut?

"Nothing," she said.

Sugar had come back again and dropped down beside Lee, who let him stay. Obviously having Sugar around was okay now.

"Tell me," he urged, absently stroking the dog's head. "I know they seemed overly interested in you."

"What?" She couldn't believe that. "They were horrible to me. They seemed only too eager to tell me the only reason you took me to the prom was that they made some silly bet with you." She lifted up her camera, giving her something to do in the silence that followed. Something to hide behind.

"*Bet?* What are you talking about?" His anger was a surprise.

"They told me why you asked me to the prom. That you only did it because they bet you to."

Lee furrowed his brow, looking as confused as she felt. "They told you I asked you out because of a bet?" He released a humorless laugh, then looked her directly in the eye, his gaze steady, his eyes narrowed as if he was trying to imprint what he was telling her. "That is not true. At all. I asked you because I wanted to."

Now it was Abby's turn to stare. "You wanted to? But…David and Mitch said that when they showed you the pictures I took of you, you laughed. And that was when they made a bet with you to ask me out. Like it was a joke."

Abby could still feel a flush of shame at the memory of taking those photographs. She was on the yearbook committee assigned to taking photos of the sports teams. She had been happy to take on the job because it gave her a legitimate reason to take pictures of Lee. She ended up with a number of great shots and had kept a couple for herself. It was those photos that David and Mitch had discovered and taunted her about. Then they had stolen them from her and told her they would show Lee.

"I did laugh when they showed me the pictures. But mostly because I was happy. I figured this meant I had a chance with you." There was a long pause. "Truth is, I'd always been attracted to you. So I certainly never asked you to the prom because Mitch or David made a *bet* with me."

She felt an unwelcome beat of anticipation mingled with confusion. "I don't understand."

Lee paused again, blowing out his breath, as if thinking. "I liked you," he said, squatting down to absently pat the dog again. "Had for a while. And, thanks to David and Mitch telling me about the pictures you took of me, I had guessed you liked me too. That's when I dared to ask you out."

"Dared to ask me out? Lee Bannister, the guy who could get most any girl in school?"

"That is not true," Lee protested.

"It is. I knew most of the girls in my class alone would have gone out with you in a heartbeat."

Lee shrugged off her comment as he sat in the straw, his back against the wall. "Well, you were the only one I had my eye on."

"Why me?" Abby still couldn't believe he was saying this. Lee had always been this elusive dream, and now he was saying he'd had his eye on her? Didn't seem possible.

"You sell yourself short. You were this amazing girl. Strong Christian. Self-confident. At least that's how it looked to me." The corner of his mouth quirked up as his gaze drifted over her. "And you were real pretty. I'd been interested in you for a while but honestly didn't think you'd want to have anything to do with me."

"Why would you think that?" she asked, a bit breathlessly.

"I knew who I was and my reputation. But I was getting sick of the life I was living and decided to just go for it when Mitch and David showed me those pictures."

It shouldn't matter so long after the fact what he said, but it was as if the air around them seemed to amplify. "Now you're just flattering me…"

"I hope so," he said, playing with Sugar's ear as the dog dropped his head on Lee's lap. Then he looked up at her, his expression intent, his dark eyes seeming to hold a banked glow. "I had a lot of fun taking you to the prom. And when you agreed to go out with me again, I figured we were moving into a good place."

Why did her heart hitch like that? She wasn't a teenager in high school anymore, yearning after one of the most sought-after guys in the valley. She was simply too aware of Lee, that was all.

"Just for curiosity, when did Mitch and David tell you all this?"

Abby thought back, surprised that she could still feel a beat of embarrassment—and sorrow—at the memory. "Just before the accident."

"Was that why you turned me down when I asked you to come to that party? Because you believed them?"

"Yes."

"But I never gave you any reason to think otherwise," he said in a low, rough voice. "Why did you think they were telling the truth?"

Abby looked down at her camera, fiddling with the settings. "I couldn't imagine that you wanted to date me," she whispered. "I guess it was easier to think you only did it because of a bet than because you chose to."

"But I did want to. And, to my shame, one of the reasons I drank too much at that party was that I was feeling sorry for myself about you."

Abby lifted her eyes to his again as old events coalesced and solidified. And as she held his steady gaze, as his words found a home in her soul, for a heart-shattering moment she wondered what would have happened if she hadn't believed Mitch and David.

"What's wrong?" Lee asked. "You look like someone just hit you."

Abby swallowed, her lips suddenly trembling,

her thoughts a whirl of bewildering emotions. "I guess I'm thinking what might have happened if I attended that party with you." She gave him a wry smile. "Maybe things would have been different. Maybe my dad..." To her embarrassment, her voice broke.

Lee pushed Sugar aside, got up and came to sit beside her. He took her hands, squeezing them firmly. "Don't you take this on," he warned her, his tone surprisingly sharp. "You did nothing wrong. What happened had *nothing* to do with you. I made my own poor choices and they...they caused what happened."

Abby didn't know what surprised her more. The intensity in his voice or how tightly he held her hands. Her heart raced with a mixture of happiness at what he said about the bet and, at the same time, a blend of guilt and pleasure at his touch.

Then the calf twitched, rustling the straw, and Lee let go of Abby's hands.

She felt suddenly disconnected and untethered. Her feelings about Lee had been complex and layered—part anger with him over her father's accident, part humiliation thinking he had only taken her out on a bet. They had become welded so tightly together that now, after his confession, she felt off-kilter and confused, unsure of how to find a new balance.

He moved to the calf, checking it over. The dog stretched, gave the calf a sniff, and then curled up between its legs as if to keep it company.

Abby snatched her camera and took refuge behind it once again. Dragging in a breath, she snapped off a few more shots of the calf with the dog, taking a couple with Lee as he put his fingers in the calf's mouth again, and then she put the lens cap on and slowly stood. She needed to go. Needed some space to sort out her conflicting emotions.

"Will he be okay?" Abby asked as she slid her camera back into her knapsack.

"I think so. I might have to tube-feed it again, but he seems to want to suck, so I might get away with bottle-feeding." Lee washed his hands in the pail of water and dried them on a towel he had taken along as well. "At least he now has Sugar to keep him company."

"So you'll have to feed it all the time now?"

He shrugged. "Yeah. But we're set up for it and once we get it used to a bottle we can transition to pail-feeding, which is quicker and easier."

Abby brushed the loose straw off her pants and shirt and slung her knapsack over her shoulder. To her consternation Lee had come a few steps closer to her, his hands strung up in his back pocket, his broad shoulders hunched forward. "Thanks for your help," he said, his voice quiet. "And thanks for listening."

Abby wasn't going to look up at him, but it was as if an invisible cord pulled her head around to face him. Once again their eyes locked as old images melded with new.

Tough Lee Bannister, wild and rebellious, kissing his mother goodbye. The man who had, she thought, hurt her in so many ways, rescuing a calf, playing with a dog, erasing shame from her past memories of him.

And now, looking at her as though he was genuinely attracted to her.

And the trouble was, she knew her old feelings for him were rekindling, changing and growing.

"I need to leave," she said, but didn't move from the spot, unable to look away from him, unable to take that first step.

"Of course," he said. But he didn't move either. Instead he brushed a remnant of straw out of her hair, his rough fingers lingering on her cheek. Abby felt as if the breath had been sucked out of her at his touch. She swallowed and fought the impulse to lean toward him.

This can't happen, she reminded herself, forcing herself to think of her mother. To think of the consequences of actions Lee had confessed to as she stepped back, then spun away.

But as she strode back to her car, she chanced another glance behind her, surprised and, at the same time, pleased to see him standing in the doorway, hands on his hips, silently watching her.

Too complicated, she thought, putting her knapsack in the car and getting in.

This can never *happen.*

"You've got the toughest hooves of any horse I've ever trimmed," Lee grumbled, pulling Rowdy's other foot up between his legs. He crouched down, catching his balance as he stabilized the hoof and reached for the hoof clippers hooked on the stand beside him.

"She's probably the worst," John agreed, leading another couple of horses out of the corral to where Lee was working. "These last two should be easier."

"I sure hope so," Lee said as he forced the clippers together, working his way around the last hoof. His back ached and sweat was pouring down his face. He'd already trimmed and shoed two horses, and he was running out of steam. "Not going to lie, right about now I'm not impressed that Kane, our usual farrier, wasn't able to come. Or that Nick decided he needed a holiday."

"Doesn't matter. Nick's no farrier and you are almost as good a farrier as Kane Hicks."

The compliment made him feel a bit better about his work.

Lee finished the last bit, set the clippers aside and slowly lowered Rowdy's foot to the ground. Then he pulled a hanky out of his back pocket and mopped the sweat off his face as he patted Rowdy on the withers. "You'll be whistling a different tune about my farrier work when you get my bill."

"I don't know how to whistle."

The sound of a car engine caught both their attention, and Lee felt a lift of his spirits when he recognized Abby's car pull up beside his truck.

"Though I think *you* could manage a whistle right about now," John joked as he lifted Clyde's hoof and began clipping.

Ignoring him, Lee stretched out the huge kink in his back, watching as Abby got out of the car. A roving breeze caught her auburn hair, tossing it around her face. The sunlight burnished it to a copper hue, and Lee's heart did a dangerous flip.

"She's beautiful, no doubt about it," John said, looking up from his work.

"I won't tell Heather you said that," Lee teased, trying to cover up his own reaction to Abby's presence.

"Stand still, you goof, or I'll tie up a leg," John warned as Clyde shifted his weight. Then he shrugged affably. "Heather told me herself she thought Abby was a looker."

"And Heather should know," Lee said wryly. John glanced over at Lee. "You may as well know. Heather thinks you two should get back together."

Lee's mind ticked back to what Abby had told him yesterday. About what Mitch and David had done to twist her perception of him and what it had done to their previous relationship. In a way it changed much, and yet the reality was, it changed nothing. Her father was still injured, her parents still divorced because of his irresponsibility.

"I would think Heather has enough other things on her mind than me and Abby."

"And what *are* your plans for the lovely Miss Newton today?" John asked with an amused grin.

"Haven't made any," he grunted as he grabbed the rasp, set Rowdy's foot on the hoof stand and began shaping and filing it. "Abby's here to interview Mom and Dad today. Get some history on the ranch and look over some of the old photos."

But at the same time, he had hoped to talk her into going out for a short ride and show her more of the ranch. At least that was his excuse.

"I imagine she'll be around for the anniversary roundup on Tuesday?"

"Of course. That's one of the reasons she's here."

It was early to move the cows from one pasture to another, but John and Monty had organized it as part of the anniversary celebrations. One of the reasons John and Lee were getting some of the horses ready.

For a few moments the only sound was the rasp of the file as Lee moved onto the last of Rowdy's hooves, the sound of John clipping, the scree of a hawk flying overhead and the occasional nicker from the horses already tied up. It was a peaceful moment, serene almost in spite of the monotonous work.

"So, where does the lovely Miss Newton go after the roundup?"

"Probably back to Seattle."

"Too bad. Sure you couldn't talk her into staying?" John ribbed. "Maybe coming to the wedding?" Lee ignored him once again, trying instead to focus on his work. Trying not to wonder if Abby would stop by here after she talked to his parents.

Then Rowdy lifted his head and nickered, looking toward the house.

Lee couldn't glance up right then, a bead of sweat dripping down his face and into his eyes as he finished the last of the rasping.

Then he heard the click and whir of a camera and he guessed Abby had come by here before going to the house. He also wondered how many pictures of him would be in this magazine article. But as he looked in her direction, he noticed she had her camera pointed to John, who was still wearing his cowboy hat, shirtsleeves rolled up, head bent over the hoof he was trimming. Clyde's head was twisted around, as if presenting his best side to Abby and the camera.

And why did the fact that she was taking John's picture make him feel jealous?

Then Abby turned to him and, as if sensing his moment of envy, snapped a few photos of him, as well.

"Hey, you," he said as he finished up, lifting Rowdy's hoof of the trimming block and setting it back on the ground. "Mom and Dad are in the house, if you're looking for them."

Abby lowered her camera and gave him a cautious smile. It was as if she wasn't sure what his reaction to her would be.

Trouble was, he wasn't sure himself. He felt as if what they had talked about yesterday had created a shift in the relationship, and he wasn't sure which direction he was allowed to go.

"I saw you guys working here and thought I'd get some shots before talking to your parents. Ranchers at work and all that." She looked away from him, down at her camera, checking her photos. "How's the calf?"

"Doing well. You want to go check on him?"

"Um, well, I'd like to, but your parents—"

"Can wait," John put in, straightening and arching his back. "You've got a stake in that critter, may as well see how he's doing."

Lee shot the other man a warning glance, but John just grinned, moved to Clyde's other hoof, picked it up and clamped it down between his legs.

"I guess I could have a look…" Abby said.

"I just have to put Rowdy in the pen and we can go."

"Does the calf need to be fed? I wouldn't mind getting a few shots of that."

"I fed him early this morning, but it wouldn't hurt to give him another feed."

Abby's grin was open and carefree, and Lee felt a thrum of anticipation as he led Rowdy back into the pen. He took the halter off, coiled it up, walked back to where Abby was waiting then latched the gate. "Let's go, then," he said, angling his head toward the barn.

Abby followed him as he strode to the room off the calving barn.

"So, you're feeding him colostrum, right?" she asked as he grabbed a pail and a bag of powder from the cupboard.

"That's correct," he said, impressed that she'd been paying attention the other day. "It's full of antibodies and all the good stuff that they need to get a good start." He began to mix the powder into the warm water. "This isn't as good as the real thing calves normally get from their mother, but it's better than straight milk, which is what he'll be getting after this feed until we can wean him."

Lee poured the warm mixture into a bottle and snapped the nipple on.

"No tube today?"

He shook his head as he led the way back to the pen. "No. That was a onetime emergency procedure. He's drinking fine now. It will be bottle feeds until we can get him to drink straight out of a pail."

The calf was on its stomach in the pen, legs curled under him, head to one side, just the way a healthy calf should be lying. Lee was about to go into the pen when he turned to Abby and held out the bottle. "So...you want to do the honors?"

Abby shook her head and held up her camera. "No, thanks. I was hoping to get some more pictures."

"I can take some of you," he offered. "Would make the article more interesting. Give it that personal touch."

Abby glanced from him to the calf, looking uncertain.

"Just put your camera on the green square," Lee said. "I'll take it from there."

Abby laughed. "How do you know about the automatic setting?"

"I took a few photography classes in prison," he said. "Some good person who liked to volunteer would come and show us how to use a camera."

Abby's gaze jerked away as silence fell like the clang of a prison door. Lee fought a surge of frustration. He really had to learn to keep that part of his life to himself.

"So, what kind of camera did you use? In your prison classes?" Abby asked as she pulled her own camera out of her ever-present backpack. "Canon? Nikon? Leica?"

"A black camera," Lee said with an attempt at levity to ease the tension between them. "With a lens."

"That narrows it down," Abby said with a grin, obviously willing to go along. "Anyway, if you're going with automatic, the flash will probably go off. That will flatten everything, so I'll set it up, let it go to autofocus and you should be okay."

"And how do you want me to frame the shot?"

"Wow. I *am* in the presence of a photography genius," Abby returned with another playful grin.

Lee felt the tension gripping him since his prison comment slowly dissipate. "I'm a renaissance man. I also know how to bake bread."

"Most impressive," Abby said. "With such a wide array of talents, I'm surprised you don't have your own blog."

"Lee Bannister dot com," he joked, moving his hand as if underlining a marquee. "Slogan, 'Sponsor him because he kneads the dough.'"

Abby's laugh was like a burst of sunshine, her sparkling eyes kindling a glimmer of hope.

And, even more, an attraction that grew with each meeting. An attraction he wasn't sure what to do about anymore.

Chapter Eight

"Are they usually this strong?" Abby asked as the calf sucked eagerly at the bottle, its mouth wrapped tightly around the nipple. She had to hang on to the bottle with both hands to keep it from getting pulled out.

"Yeah. And it gets worse when they get older and bigger and start to bunt. That's why we move to feeding them out of a pail as soon as possible."

Abby stole a quick glance over her shoulder at Lee, but the camera hid his face. "You can stop taking pictures now," she said with a nervous laugh. "You must have enough." She wasn't accustomed to being on this side of the lens, and it made her feel vulnerable.

Especially because it was Lee taking her photo. After the confessions of yesterday, she felt as if much had been reshaped between her and Lee. Last night she had stared at a watermark in the ceiling for what seemed like hours, going over what they had talked about. Knowing that he had wanted to take her out, that he was distraught that she had spurned him before that fateful party, had given her a different perspective on Lee.

A perspective that bothered and thrilled her at the same time.

"Easy to be bossy from your side of the camera," Lee muttered, seeming to ignore her as he fired off a few more shots.

"Seriously, Lee, you've got enough," she said, turning her attention back to the calf, who was still tugging for all it was worth at the bottle. A few more sucks and it was empty. Abby pulled it out of the calf's mouth, but it was a momentary tug of war. Finally he released it.

"You might want to step back," Lee cautioned as he fired off a few more shots.

"Why?"

The calf shook its head, remnant drops of milk flying, jumped back, then began bucking its legs going every which way.

Alarmed, Abby retreated to a corner of the pen. "What's going on?"

"People usually like to sit after a warm meal, whereas calves seem to get all lively and frisky. Trouble is, they're not aware of anyone or anything else and you could get kicked." Lee had joined Abby in the corner, watching the calf hopping around the pen.

"Can I see what you got?" she asked, itching to get her hands on the camera.

"Sure." Lee unhooked it and was about to give it to her when the calf let out a bellow and raced across the pen.

Directly toward them.

"Watch out," Lee shouted, grabbing Abby by the arm and pulling her back. Unprepared, Abby was thrown off balance. The bottle flew out of her hands and she stumbled. Her ankle, still tender, gave way and she fell against Lee.

Still holding the camera, Lee pulled her steady with his free arm, but as he took a step back, he caught his legs on a bale of hay behind him and together they collapsed in a tangled heap to the straw-covered floor.

The calf stopped just short of them, turned its head to one side as if examining them, then raced off to the other side of the pen.

Lee was laughing and Abby couldn't help laughing herself as she tried to extricate herself from Lee's arms. But her one arm was trapped under him and he was trying to roll over, yet his leg had twisted under him somehow.

"Your camera. Sorry," he managed as he moved to one side, still grasping the camera.

He set it aside in the straw as he attempted to get up.

"It'll be fine," she said, trying to get up, as well. "It's had worse falls."

But her arm was still pinned under him and his legs were still up on the bale. They struggled, laughed some more and then Lee was up on one elbow, looking down at her. Her one hand was on his shoulder to steady herself. She could feel the warmth of his skin through the material. Their eyes met, the moment lengthened and Abby couldn't look away. She could see the golden flecks in his deep brown eyes and the thick fringe of lashes framing them.

Then to her surprise, Lee reached up and brushed her hair away from her face. As yesterday's, it was the lightest of touches, but it created a quiver of anticipation and a more troubling yearning.

Her breath was caught in her throat as she veered between the need to move and the desire to have time stop right here.

"Abby," Lee whispered.

She lifted her free hand and rested it on his cheek, the faint stubble rough under her hand. She stroked his face with her thumb, slowly, drawing the moment out, yet knowing she should leave.

Just stay for a while. You deserve this moment with him.

The voice from her past eased into the now, and her more practical self knew she should stop this.

But the loneliness that had dogged her for so many years kept her hand in place, kept her looking up at him as if the sight and touch of him could fill that emptiness deep in her soul.

And then, as if it was the only way to end to this moment, Lee lowered his head and his lips touched hers. Gently at first. Then more firmly.

Abby wrapped her hand around his neck, returning his kiss, her heart singing, all the sorrows of the past few years erased by this one moment with Lee.

He was the first to pull away and Abby protested lightly. But he stayed where he was, tracing her features with his finger. He released a slow smile, which didn't help her heart rate but made her smile in return. Then he laid his forehead against hers, his face becoming a blur. "So, Abby Newton, now what?"

His question was like a chill breeze, tugging at her fantasy.

She slowly released her hold on him and gingerly eased away. "I don't know," she said, sitting up, pulling her legs toward her and wrapping her arms around them as if protecting herself.

Lee shoved his hand through his hair as he pulled himself up to sit beside her, leaning back against the pen. He picked up her camera and toyed idly with it, as if to buy some time.

"Neither do I," he admitted. "I just know you've been taking up a lot of space in my brain lately. And last night, I kept thinking about what you told me." He folded the strap of her camera over, then uncreased it and folded it the other way. "Thinking about what Mitch and David said to you." He then looked over at her, concern etched on his handsome features. "Do you believe me when I tell you that they were lying?"

Abby held his gaze, heard the worry in his deep voice and nodded. "Yes, I believe you."

Old emotions and memories superimposed themselves over the present and Abby felt, once again, the rush of attraction Lee could always create in her. Except now she felt a change. He wasn't simply the guy she had a crush on. He was the man who had changed her life.

But he paid for that.

Yes, he had, but his shadow still lay over her life.

Forgive as the Lord forgave you.

Abby lowered her head to her knees, trying to still the competing thoughts. In spite of the accident, even in spite of what David and Mitch had told her, a part of her heart had always been reserved for Lee. And it was that part reasoning with her now. Telling her that all she had wanted was right here. Finally within reach.

"I'm sorry," he said huskily. "I know it's always the wrong thing to say after a guy kisses a girl, but I feel like I stepped over the line."

Abby lifted her head and looked directly at him, holding his gaze, looking for an answer to her dilemma.

His dark eyes were anguished and his expression made her want to reach out and touch him. Reassure him.

"You didn't step over any line that I laid down," she whispered. Then, fearing she would do something more foolish, she took her camera from him, got up and left.

Lee tapped the last nail into Tia's hoof, lowered it to the ground. As he stretched the kink out of his back, he looked back toward the house. Abby was still inside, speaking with his parents.

"Obviously they've got lots to talk about," John said, catching the direction of Lee's gaze.

"One hundred and fifty years of ranching," Lee muttered, picking up Tia's hoof again, grabbing the clench and bending over the nails he had just put in.

John was in the corrals when he and Abby

had come out of the barn. Good thing that Heather's fiancé was one of those quiet, discreet types, because Lee was sure he had to have noticed something.

He set the hoof on the hoof stand, then rasped and filed the ends of the nails sticking out of the hooves, half his attention on his work, the other half on the ranch house where Abby's car was still parked.

She had been there as long as he'd been working on the horses, which was about an hour now.

"So, that's the last of it," Lee said, taking Tia's hoof off the stand. "All horses are shoed and ready for Tuesday."

"Can't believe it's here already," John remarked. "Feel like we've been getting ready for months for all this."

"Keira and Tanner sure made everyone busy having the wedding the same week as the anniversary." Lee was surprised Heather and John had decided not to make it a double wedding with Keira and Tanner, but Heather had said she'd already had the big splash with her first wedding to Mitch. She wanted a smaller, quieter ceremony later and she didn't want to take anything away from her sister's big day.

"Figured it was the best way to get you here," John replied with a grin, dropping his rasp into the box he'd been using. "Besides, some of the people coming for the anniversary will be here for the wedding too. All the relatives anyway."

Though Monty was an only child, his father, like Lee, had grown up with two sisters, both of whom had moved away from Saddlebank. One great-aunt was still single, too outspoken to get married, she always said. The other had moved to Missoula, wed a dentist and had four children, all of them now married, as well. The rest of the relatives were great-uncles and aunts, most of whom Lee hadn't seen in years and barely knew. And they would all be descending on the ranch, en mass, come Tuesday.

Lee led Tia back into the pasture, shooting another glance over his shoulder at the house. He came back to the corrals, tugged his gloves off and stuffed them in his back pocket. He was sweaty and hot and needed to wash up.

"Coming to the house?" John asked, closing the gate behind him.

"In a bit. I want to check on the calf first."

"He's fine." John gave him a sly grin. "Thought you might be eager to go and see Miss Newton again. What with you two rolling in the straw just an hour or so ago."

Lee shot him an incensed glance. "What are you talking about?"

John walked over and plucked a few wisps of straw off Lee's head. "Well, looky here, if these don't exactly match the ones I just saw in Miss Newton's hair," he drawled.

"We were feeding the calf. He got frisky."

"Calf's not the only one that got frisky," John said, adding a broad wink.

Lee felt a flush creep up his neck.

"Hey, I don't blame you," the other man continued. "As I mentioned before, she's a beautiful woman. And from what I see, she seems to think you're fairly easy on the eyes, as well. At least, the way she looks at you I'm guessing she does."

Lee pulled in a long breath, realizing he could hide nothing from his future brother-in-law. "You know who she is and our history."

"Yeah. I do."

"It can't happen. The situation is complicated."

"That's what I thought about me and Heather," John said. "I had Adana to think about. A wife I was supposed to be mourning. Heather was divorced from an abusive man. I thought it was too messy. Too complicated. But we fell in love and love seems to find its own way through the complications."

Lee heard the sincerity in John's voice and wanted to believe it.

"What I did to her family can't be forgiven," he bit out.

"That's your opinion," John said, dropping an assuring hand on his shoulder. "But at the risk of sounding like a walking cliché, with God all things are possible. I know you are genuinely sorry. That you've asked forgiveness from God, from her family." He cleared his throat. "You paid for that mistake. I think, in some ways, you're still paying for it. I know you truly regret what happened. Let her know that."

"I have," Lee replied.

"Then trust that if she understands she'll see you for the man you've become, not the man you were."

Lee thought of the moments, the kiss he and Abby had shared. Though she had expressed her difficulty with him and with forgiving him, at the same time she hadn't spurned him.

"You look like you don't believe me," John said.

Lee leaned back against the fence, crossing his arms over his chest. "I'd like to, but I feel like I need time to process everything. My life has been chaos for too many years. I guess I'm just worn out."

"I'm not surprised. You're working a job you don't like, keeping yourself away from your family and your community with some mistaken notion that you have to punish yourself for what you did."

"I'm not punishing myself."

"Then why don't you come back?" John asked, a note of challenge in his voice. "Why don't you take your place as a co-owner of the ranch?"

Lee shot him a puzzled frown. "But you're partners with Dad now. You don't need me."

"Monty isn't getting any younger and we've been increasing the herd every year, holding calves back, calving out more heifers every year. In fact, we've been looking at hiring a couple more hands this fall when we bring the calves in." John dropped his hands on his hips, holding Lee's gaze, his own steady. "You know you belong here. Even in the few days you've been here, I've seen you drop that reserve you wrap around yourself. You look happy and content."

John grew silent for a few moments, as if to let it all sink in. Finally he said, "Think about it, Lee. I think the ranch fills a space in you that's been empty since you left."

Then, after throwing all that at him, John turned and walked back to the ranch house.

Lee slowly looked around the ranch, letting thoughts tease him as his future brother-in-law's words took root in his soul.

Coming back? Was it even possible? Did he deserve it?

He pushed himself away from the fence, stifling those thoughts for now. He could only look to the next few days and his obligations.

Yet, as he neared the house, his heart lifted in anticipation. The door opened and Abby stepped outside, calling out her goodbyes to his parents. She looked so beautiful, standing there, the sun glinting off her red hair, burnishing her complexion. She shut the door, then paused, as if her thoughts were elsewhere. Then she gave her head a shake, turned and jumped when she saw Lee approach.

"Hey there," he said quietly, stopping in front of her. Close enough to see the flush that reddened her cheeks.

"Hey yourself."

Lee swallowed, fighting the impulse to touch her. Stroke her cheek. Try to steal another kiss. He couldn't be sure his parents weren't watching.

"So, you done with the interview?"

She nodded, looking down at the notebook she was clutching. "Got lots of information. I just need to clean it all up and input it on the computer."

Was it his imagination or did she sound as breathless as he felt?

Then she looked up at him and he caught a look of yearning that called to his own.

"Hey," he whispered. Then he gave in to his

impulse, reached out and cupped her cheek. "I think we need to talk."

"Probably," she returned. Then, to his pleasant surprise, she caught his hand in her own, holding it against her face. She gave him a gentle smile, then stepped away. "But for now, I need space. Some thinking time."

Lee didn't like the sound of that, but nonetheless, he didn't blame her. He knew he had to do the same.

She brushed her hand over his arm, then walked away to her car.

As Lee watched her drive off, he wondered what would happen next between them.

Could he and Abby do this? Could they overcome all the odds stacked against them?

Chapter Nine

"Forgiveness, one of the more misunderstood words in the Bible, is what the Bible is all about," Pastor Dykstra said, looking over the congregation of the Saddlebank Community Church. "Our forgiveness from God does not depend on what we do, but on who God is." He paused and Abby caught herself glancing over at Lee Bannister, sitting across the aisle and a couple of pews ahead of her.

"Forgiveness does not mean forgetting," the pastor continued, pulling her attention back to him. "Scars will always remain. But true forgiveness, the kind that God grants us, swallows pride and is willing to see the other person as God does. Flawed, but free. To quote Frederich Buechner, 'When you forgive somebody who has wronged you, you're spared the dismal corrosion of bitterness and wounded pride.' These are words we need to take to heart."

Abby let his words seep into her soul, and, in spite of her mother's feelings toward the Bannisters, felt the bonds holding her heart captive loosening.

She knew her mother had to find her own way through this situation. Like the quote the pastor had just recited, her mother was feeling that same corrosion of bitterness. But Abby couldn't carry the burden of her mother's feelings any longer.

You're only thinking that because you're starting to care for Lee.

The insidious voice intruded, creating hesitation. But as Abby looked down at the Bible again, rereading the passage Pastor Dykstra had based his sermon on—the man who owed the king thousands, unable to forgive the debt of his servant who, in turn, owed him pennies—she realized she had her own unpayable debts. The fact was, she couldn't stand before God with a pure heart either. She needed to be forgiven much and could do no less.

Emotion swept through her as she finally faced the undeniable truth. She was tired of bitterness and anger and she didn't want it taking up her life a second longer. It had held her captive for far too long. Then, as she opened her eyes, it was as if a weight slipped off her shoulders. She was allowed to forgive Lee. And although it might have seemed unthinkable before, she finally understood that she didn't need to drag her mother's condemnation along with her.

Abby returned her attention back to Pastor Dykstra. When he gave them the benediction after the final song, she felt a peace pervade her life she hadn't felt in years.

She couldn't help the smile wreathing her lips and as she stepped into the aisle, that smile grew wider when Lee found his way to her.

"So you decided to join us after all?" he asked, tucking his worn Bible under one arm, his other hand brushing her arm as he walked alongside her.

"I did," she said, darting a quick glance up at him, then away, his featherlight touch sending a shiver dancing down her spine. "And I'm glad I did. The sermon…well…it seemed appropriate."

Lee slanted her a crooked smile. "I think when you're seeking, God will find a way to speak to you."

He sounded earnest and she realized that, for Lee, his faith had become the bedrock of his existence. Which made him, suddenly, even more appealing.

Then, to her surprise, Lee gently took her

arm, leading her to one side of the foyer, away from the people exiting the sanctuary.

"My parents and I were wondering if you and your mother wanted to join us for lunch," he said. "I know you've spent a lot of your extra time at the ranch, but we'd love to have you for a social visit. You can leave the camera and notebook at home."

Abby felt a flutter of excitement at the thought of spending more time with Lee. But superimposed over that was the picture of her mother coming to Refuge Ranch. Having lunch with the Bannisters. She shook her head. "I'd love to come, but I don't think my mom is ready for a visit to the ranch." Especially not if Lee would be there.

Lee's hopeful expression faltered with her comment. "Of course. I understand."

Anticipation and reality hummed between them, neither of them willing to leave as the last of the congregation walked past them. She knew it wasn't simply her overactive imagination that stirred these feelings.

You've always been a beautiful person, inside and out.

Oh, how closely she had held these words. Taken them out like a secret treasure to savor. And now she wanted nothing more than to move closer and let him put his arms around her.

"Will you be coming to the ranch tomorrow?" he asked, eking the conversation out.

"No. I need to work on some of the pictures and edit them. I want to have everything ready to go when the article is done."

"Which will be after the anniversary celebration."

Abby nodded, feeling a sudden flutter of concern. What would happen after that? She wasn't asking and it seemed Lee was as unsure as she was.

She looked up at him, his dark eyes fixed on hers, his mouth tipped up at one corner in a rueful smile.

"Lee, you two coming?" Keira called out from below.

"Sorry," Lee said, with an apologetic smile. "She seems to assume you'll be coming, as well."

"Give her my regrets."

Lee nodded, touched her arm lightly as if to say goodbye, then turned and left. Abby watched him go, confusion and yearning knotted around each other. She wanted to put them aside, but all the way to the Grill and Chill, all she could think about was Lee. And how she wished she was going to the ranch instead of meeting Louisa and her mother for lunch.

A short time later, Abby pulled up in front

of the café and dialed her mother's number. Ivy hadn't come to church, pleading a headache. Abby suspected it had much to do with Lee's presence there.

"Hey, Mom, how are you doing?" she asked with a forced cheer when her mother answered the phone. "How is the headache?"

"It's getting worse," Ivy said, sounding strained. "Your father called while you were in church."

"Oh no." Abby sighed. "Does he still say he wants to talk to you? What did you tell him?"

"I said I wasn't sure."

Abby wanted to tell her mother to tell him no. But at the same time she could hear the faintest tremor of hope in her mother's voice.

"So you won't be meeting me and Louisa?" she asked.

"Sorry, honey. No."

"I'll come home, then," Abby said, pulling her keys out of her purse.

"Don't do that. I just want to sleep." Ivy was quiet a moment. "How was church?"

"Good. I was glad I went."

"Was Lee there?" her mom asked.

"Yes. He was."

"Doesn't seem right, does it? He's the one that did wrong, yet he comes back to his intact family, his ranch and beautiful home. You come back to a mother who has to work and who fights headaches."

The faint bitterness in her mother's voice re-awakened a swarm of contradictory emotions. The usual guilt over her attraction to Lee and behind that a sense that she had to choose what to take on and what to leave behind.

When you forgive somebody...you're spared the dismal corrosion of bitterness.

As the pastor's words sifted back into her mind, Abby felt a gentle release. A separation from her mother's pain and sorrow. She had forgiven Lee for what had happened to her. Her mother had to find her own way through all this.

"Make sure you get some rest." She ended the call, then dropped her phone into her purse, pressing her fingers to her temples as if to anchor her thoughts. "Help me to reconcile all this on my own," she prayed. "Help me to know that forgiveness is not giving in. I want to be free of this burden. I want to let go. Help my mother to be free as well and help me not to take on her pain."

That being said, she felt sorry for her mother. Which made her think about her father calling her mom. It wasn't fair. Why would he do that to her after all this time?

Suddenly her phone rang, startling her out of

her thoughts, and her heart sank when she saw who it was who was calling.

Her father.

She hesitated to answer it, struggling to find her way through the mine field of other people's expectations. Then, swallowing a lump in her throat, she finally hit the phone button to accept the call and sent up another prayer. "Hello, Abby," Cornell said quietly. "I haven't heard from you in a while. How you been doing?"

"Been doing good," Abby said, wrapping one arm around her middle, her reactions fighting with each other.

She missed him.

She was angry with him.

She felt sorry for him.

What he had become was a direct result of the accident, but he had a choice and he had made some wrong ones.

"Good. Good. I hear you're working for the Bannisters."

"Not working *for* them. I'm doing a piece about them for the magazine I write for. That's all." She wasn't sure why she felt she had to qualify that statement. Especially after the epiphany she'd had at church this morning. "It's the ranch's hundred and fiftieth anniversary."

"How is the ranch doing?"

Abby frowned, wondering why he asked this. "Good, as far as I know."

"So they're not broke, then."

"Far from it," Abby said.

"Glad to hear that."

Goodness, he wasn't going to go ask them for more money, was he? Abby stifled a quell of panic at the thought.

"And I hear Lee is back? He okay?" Cornell asked.

More than okay, Abby thought, a faint smile curling her lips. "He's fine, Dad. Why do you want to know?"

"Well, I always felt bad for him, that's all."

Her father's comment baffled her, considering the bitterness that had consumed him after the accident. "And your mom…she's not doing so well?"

"No. She says that when you call it bothers her. She gets headaches."

Her father sighed. "I'm sorry to hear that."

"Why do you keep calling her?"

"I want to talk to her and I want to talk to you. That's why I finally called. You need to know I've changed, honey. I'm not drinking anymore. I know what I did was wrong. I mean, to your mother."

Abby breathed a small sigh of relief at her father's confession. It helped ease some of the strain she always felt—torn between the sympathy she felt for her father and yet knowing that his actions had caused the divorce that ripped her life apart.

"I'm glad you see that, Dad. Look, I gotta go. I'm meeting Louisa."

"Of course. I'd like to talk to you sometime. Soon." And then her father said goodbye and hung up.

That was a bewildering phone call, Abby thought, biting her lip. But she put it behind her and walked over to the diner, looking forward to her visit with her friend. Once inside, she scanned the upper portion of the café and saw Louisa at the very back, in one of the booths, waving at her.

"Hey, you, where's your mom?" Louisa asked as Abby slipped into the bench across from her.

"Headache. Dad's been phoning."

"That's tough. Does he say what he wants?"

"To talk to her. I just spoke to him too, but I don't want to talk about that now, okay?"

"Have it your way," Louisa replied, a frown knitting her brow.

Hoping her friend would leave it at that, Abby grabbed the laminated menu lying on the worn, wooden table. Marks and gouges from previous customers were etched into its finish. The Grill and Chill had been part of Saddlebank for decades, and although the current owner had modernized and fixed it up, he had kept parts of the old restaurant intact to maintain a comfortable ambience.

Abby looked over the menu, surprised. "Wow. George has really expanded his culinary horizons. I don't think I've ever seen this many salads on the menu."

"Apparently he started when Brooke stopped eating here and started going to Pat's Place. I think he was hoping to lure her back."

"Are those two dating?"

"Apparently, no. But who knows? I think the people of Saddlebank live in hope."

Brooke Dillon and George Bamford's on-again, off-again relationship was a never-ending source of Saddlebank gossip.

Their waitress, Allison Bamford, came by and poured them each a coffee. Then Louisa ordered her usual Cobb salad and Abby ordered a burger and fries.

"Really?" Louisa scoffed. "With all these lovely salad choices, you order a burger? You're such a carnivore."

"I didn't claw my way up the food chain to eat roughage," Abby said. "Besides, I didn't have breakfast. My stomach was rumbling so loud during church I thought the usher was going to escort me out."

"So, how was church?" Louisa asked, resting her elbows on the table and taking a sip of her coffee.

"I enjoyed going again. They have a good pastor here." She smiled, thinking of what she had learned this morning.

"So I need to ask," Louisa said with a smirk. "What was the bigger draw for church? A deep need to reconnect with the faith of your childhood, or Lee Bannister?"

Abby shot her friend an annoyed look as she dumped a sugar packet in her coffee. "I wanted to go for myself. And like you said, I wanted to reconnect with the faith of my childhood."

"But Lee was there."

"Yes."

"Looks like he's reconnecting with the faith of his childhood too," Louisa said, flashing her a knowing smile.

"Probably. He told me that he found his faith again in prison."

Louisa could see that her friend was weighing this information. "Do you think he's sincere?"

"I think he is. If it was simply the foxhole Christian effect, I'm sure it would have worn off. But he seems to have hung on to it." It hadn't been hard to see that sincerity in how he listened to the pastor. How he sang the songs and followed along in the Bible when the pastor read.

"At least he cut loose from Mitch and David. 'Course David's dead, so that wasn't hard." Louisa winced. "Sorry. That sounded a bit insensitive."

"David reaped what he sowed." Abby pressed her finger on the loose granules of sugar that had fallen from her sugar packet. She didn't care about Mitch and David's reputation, but she wanted to clear Lee's name with Louisa. "You know, Lee never made any bet with Mitch and David about taking me to the prom," she said quietly. "Lee told me he went out with me because he wanted to. Mitch and David were just being jerks when they told me about a bet."

Louisa was the first person Abby had turned to when Mitch and David gleefully shattered her illusions about Lee. No sooner had Louisa heard than she marched over to Lee and gave him a piece of her mind.

"Again, do you believe it?" Louisa looked and sounded skeptical and, in a way, Abby couldn't blame her. In spite of Lee's confession, his overall behavior in high school had been less than stellar.

"Why would he lie?" Abby held her friend's steady gaze. "He has nothing to gain by that."

"Except to make himself look better to you."

"Well, I believe him," Abby said, trying not to feel like she was slowly getting pushed into a corner. She already knew how her mother felt about Lee; it would have been nice to get some support from her friend.

"Actually, I believe him too," Louisa admitted with a wry grin. "I'm kind of glad that he wasn't the scoundrel I thought he was. I know he liked you in high school." She winked. "I could see the way he used to look at you."

"I never received that impression from you before. I thought you didn't like him."

"Full disclosure? I was probably a bit jealous. He's one handsome man, all dark-eyed and broody-looking. And now that he's let that thick, dark hair grow out..." Louisa released an overly dramatic sigh, looking all dreamy-eyed. "Anyhow, I think it's great that you two are getting together again. I know you always liked him."

"I'm not sure about the getting-together part," Abby said, giving her friend a warning look as Allison set their plates of food in front of them. Louisa took the hint and murmured her thanks, waiting until the waitress was out of earshot.

"So he's not attracted to you anymore?"

Abby thought of the kiss they had shared. The nearly electric moment in church just an hour ago.

"You're blushing!" Louisa said, leaning forward with an anticipatory grin. "Spill."

Abby swiped a french fry through her ketchup, buying herself some time to gather her composure. "We had…a moment. Or two. Maybe more."

"No. Way." Louisa's grin widened. "Kissing?"

Abby couldn't help smiling at Louisa's avid interest.

"Okay, you're not saying, but you don't have to. You're redder than that mound of ketchup on your plate." Louisa stabbed a forkful of lettuce. "So, what are you going to do about this? You'll be done with the job at the Bannisters' after Tuesday. Unless you want to do some follow-up. Which, given what you just told me, is more than likely. But then what?"

Abby shrugged, her friend's comment bringing her plummeting back to reality. "I don't know. Maddie's a great boss, but to be perfectly honest, I haven't enjoyed my job for a while now. I'm tired of traveling. And as far as Lee is concerned…"

"Everything is a maybe," Louisa finished for her. "A possibility."

"Lee has a job he has to go back to, as well. I don't know what his plans are. Don't know if I have any right to be involved in them or to have expectations."

"But you'd like to," Louisa surmised, then took another bite of her salad. Abby toyed with her fries, suddenly not as hungry as she thought.

"I hate uncertainty," she said suddenly. "And I don't want my life to be determined by someone else's decisions."

Abby had had enough of that happen in her life. She didn't know if she could allow it again.

"So, you manage to get some good people shots?" Lee asked, watching as Abby switched her lens on her camera.

The sun had cooperated for the day of the anniversary and was shining brightly though Abby had grumbled about how a bit of cloud would have been nice for taking pictures.

Abby looked past him at the gathering of people and dignitaries. "I sure hope so. I kind of feel like paparazzi walking around with my camera in front of my face all the time."

The mayor of Saddlebank stood just a ways away from them chatting up the mayor of Bozeman. Just past them Lee could see the state's governor listening to his aunt, her voice carrying over the yard. Lee had been circulating through the gathered crowd, catching up with old relatives and trying to make conversation with people who were part of his youth and whose names he barely remembered.

He was fairly sure they remembered him. His distant relative Keith McCauley, former sheriff of Saddlebank County, had made a few gruff comments in passing.

"I just hope I don't end up with too many shadowed faces." Abby stowed the other lens in a case and slipped it in her backpack. She had a small notebook that she had scribbled some notes in while the family was lingering over coffee in the house this morning. It had been fun to watch her talk to her parents, to John and Keira and Heather, drawing out their stories of other roundups. How it was done in the past and possibly what could change for the future.

She had also been working her way through the crowd the past half hour, chitchatting with people. Lee could see she had a way of putting folks at ease. A quiet about her that made others want to confide in her.

They now stood close to the area set aside for the presentations and the few speeches that would be made by the invited dignitaries.

"Did you see the camera crew here from a television station in Bozeman? Is that okay with you?"

"It's fine." She smiled but behind that he sensed some misgivings. Ever since she came this morning, he felt as if she had put distance between them. He wasn't sure what caused it, but he was determined to find out. Because he didn't want any misunderstandings. Not now.

Yesterday the whole family had been busy with preparations for today—mowing lawns, weeding flower beds, setting out tables and cleaning up the outbuildings—but in spite of the flurry of activity, he missed Abby. Every vehicle that came on the yard made him look up with a sense of expectation, but she stayed away.

Thankfully she was here first thing in the morning, right after they were done with breakfast.

Now his parents stood to one side of the podium Tanner and Lee had made yesterday, going over the speeches they had prepared. The girls were walking around, welcoming the people who had shown up, offering refreshments from the buffet table sitting to one side of the open area designated for the celebration. Two huge decorated cakes rested on the table, flanked by plates of squares and cookies. Bouquets of lilies, wild roses, laveteria and potato vine gathered from his mother's extensive flower garden filled old metal pails set on each side of the podium. A rustic arbor made of willow branches created a backdrop.

Meanwhile, John and Tanner were in the corrals getting the horses ready to go. Adana was with her other grandparents who were by the corrals, watching as John worked. It was all coming together. Fifteen more minutes and the festivities would officially begin.

Which meant Lee didn't have a second to waste if he wanted to get to the bottom of what was going on with Abby.

"Is everything okay?" he asked her, taking her arm and gently drawing her aside. "You seem distant."

"I have stuff on my mind," she said softly, fiddling with her camera and lifting it to take a photo of the gathering. "I'll be done with all the work on this magazine article after today. So I'll be finished here."

"Of course."

"And, I imagine, you'll have to get back to work too." She lowered her camera, giving him a cautious smile.

He knew uncertainty marred their relationship. But he felt he had to at least let her know where he was at. Just for information, he reminded himself, no other reason.

"I'm not sure what to do," he said.

Hitching in a breath, she looked up at him. "You shouldn't turn your back on all this." She waved her hand around the yard, encompassing the house, the barns, corrals and outbuildings that had been constantly upgraded and updated. He himself had pounded many nails, attached many staples, ridden many miles over this place. "It's a heritage and you're blessed to have it."

He held her gaze. The passion in her voice matched his feelings about the ranch. He wanted to stay, but he wanted Abby to, as well. However, he couldn't come right out and say that. Always hovering over their relationship was what he had done to her father.

But he couldn't let her walk away.

Then Monty stepped up to the microphone attached to the dais, and Abby started snapping photos. Back to work for her.

His dad tapped the mike to check for sound and then he leaned forward. "Well, I think we can get started," he said, his voice booming over the gathering.

People stopped what they were doing and conversation drifted into silence. Lee walked over to where his family stood, taking his place by his mother. He dropped his arm over her shoulder and gave her a quick one-armed hug. "Here we go," he whispered.

"I'm so thankful you're here," his mother whispered back, covering his hand with hers. She looked past him to where Abby stood on the edge of the crowd, taking pictures. "And while I had my reservations about her, I'm very thankful Abby is doing this piece. She's a wonderful girl. I hope we can see more of her once this whole celebration is over."

Lee rolled his eyes. *Subtle* wasn't a word in Ellen Bannister's vocabulary, but he wasn't getting pulled into his mother's web.

"I think Dad wants to start," he said, nodding toward his father, who stood at the podium. "You better go join him."

His mother gave him a wink, then walked over to his father.

They stood side by side, his father tall and robust, his hair still thick and wavy. He wore a white shirt and a new tie in honor of this occasion, a pair of brand-new blue jeans, but had insisted on wearing his worn, slant-heeled cowboy boots.

Ellen had on a simple pink dress and was wearing a Montana silver necklace with coral insets that had been passed on through the family. Her gray hair glinted in the sun, framing her face.

Still so beautiful, Lee thought as his mother took his father's arm. Monty gazed down on her and gave her that special smile he always reserved for her.

"This is a momentous day for the Bannister family," Monty said, turning back to the crowd composed of friends, neighbors and a few dignitaries. "It's not many businesses that last one hundred and fifty years. But Refuge Ranch has endured because it is so much more than a business. It's a legacy. A trust that has been passed down through our family through many, many generations. Ranching is not what you do, it's who you are, and I've been thankful to be a rancher from the day I was born on this ranch, as was my father and his father before him.

"I grew up on this place and have always been taught that no one person owns this place. It has been given to whoever comes after in trust to take care of and pass on. And through all the generations of ranching on Refuge Ranch, God has been faithful, bringing us through storms and drought. Through varying cattle prices. Through catastrophes and wars and depressions and recessions and booming markets and disease. We know that we, as a family, are blessed to have this legacy and, Lord willing, it will continue."

Lee felt his heart fill with pride at his father's words.

He looked out over the ranch again—the fields green and lush, flowing toward the hills, then the craggy mountains beyond—feeling the land calling to him. This was his home. This was where he was meant to be.

He stole a glance over at Abby, who had lowered her camera and was watching his father as if also absorbing what he had to say. She took a few more pictures, and then her eyes found his.

Across the crowd he held her gaze, unable to look away.

He belonged here, that much he knew.

He just wished he knew where Abby fit in all this. And would she? Could she completely let go of what he had done? Would she be willing to be a part of his life?

Brown bodies plodded ahead of Abby, heads down, bawling occasionally as they walked along the wide lane, fences on either side. They seemed too spread out, but Tanner, riding in the rear of the herd, assured her that it was better that way. Cattle didn't like to get crowded. So they only let out a few at a time from the pasture they'd been gathering them from to give them their space.

She got a few good shots of them off the back of Bonny and on the ground when the crew who had come to help had gathered animals from the various parts of the pasture. It had taken longer than she thought. Animals veered off into hills and draws and local cowboys cantered off to herd them back. Everyone seemed to be having fun, and in the process Abby met a few of Lee's relatives who had joined in the pasture move.

But now the cattle seemed to be ambling

along so she put her camera away, satisfied with the pictures she had already taken. She would grab more at the end of the move. She just wanted to enjoy being outside, riding a horse.

But even more enjoyable was watching Lee. He looked happy. Content. At peace.

He waved his coiled-up rope, nudged his horse and cantered up the side of the herd, prodding a cow who was trying to turn back. He looked so at ease on the horse. So at one with it, his movements so natural and smooth.

As if aware of her scrutiny, he looked back over his shoulder and waved his rope at her. She wasn't sure what he wanted, but her horse seemed to. It broke into a trot, heading directly toward Lee. She bounced in the saddle, trying to get a rhythm going, but it was no use. She couldn't look as relaxed as he or the others did.

"How are you doing?" Lee asked as she came up alongside him.

"Good, except I feel like a complete urbanite."

"What do you mean by that?" He tugged his hat farther down on his head, squinting at the lead cows, who seemed to be slowing down.

"Even your relatives ride better than I do," Abby grumbled, shifting in the saddle, muscles from her previous ride still tender.

"You'll learn," he said with an encouraging smile.

His comment—a simple assumption that she would be around to gain enough experience to master horseback riding—gave her a small thrill. But right behind that came the usual questions about what would happen after today.

Yesterday she had stayed away, working on her article and photos, but every minute, every picture of Lee, made her want to shut her laptop off and come directly here.

"So, what happens when we get nearer the pasture where the cows are supposed to be?" Abby asked, changing the topic to keep her mind in the moment. To keep questions about tomorrow at bay.

"Nothing dramatic," Lee said. "We open the gate and let them in."

"Really? That's all?"

"Afraid so."

"I thought you would be branding or something like that."

"Sorry to disappoint you." The corner of his mouth quirked up. "That was already done this spring before we put the calves out to pasture the first time."

"Too bad I missed that," she said. "That would have been a great addition to the piece."

"Maybe next time," he said.

And there it was again. A quiet assumption of a progression in the relationship.

"So, how do your father and John manage to handle all these cows by themselves?"

"They have Nick hired. But in the spring, during branding season, a few other ranchers have been sending in their hands to come and help. Since John signed on, they've been increasing the herd and I know they're talking about hiring a few more full-time hands. They're going to need more help if they keep expanding."

"Can they? Expand more?"

Nodding slowly, he replied, "Dad has managed to hang on to a lot of leased land that he hasn't utilized since…well, since I left. He has lots of room to increase the herd. And right now cattle prices are good, so the cash flow is healthy."

And would he stay? Help his father out?

The questions stayed where they belonged: in one corner of her mind. It wasn't her business. She had her own plans.

Then Lee glanced her way. Though his eyes were shadowed by the brim of his hat, Abby could feel his attention, as if he sensed her questions. As if he had questions of his own. Trouble was, she wasn't sure herself what she wanted anymore. She felt a curious sense of settling as she looked away from him, comparing these wide-open spaces to the cramped apartment she shared with Louisa. The busy streets of Seattle, the endless traveling she did from place to place.

She had no home, she realized with a pang. No place where she felt she belonged. Being here, at Refuge Ranch, was the first time she truly felt a sense of home.

She brushed the maudlin thoughts aside, reminding herself that, for now, she was in a good place, doing something enjoyable with someone she liked being with.

But will you be able to leave?

The question twisted her heart as she snuck a look at Lee again. What was she allowed to assume? This man had such an influence on her past. Did she dare put her future in his hands?

Chapter Ten

The fire crackled and snapped, illuminating the faces of the people circling it, sending sparks spiraling up as if to touch the complacent full moon, hanging in the sky overhead. Conversation flowed, punctuated by bursts of laughter as stories were exchanged and memories revisited.

A caterer had followed the cattle drive with a wagon stocked with firewood, hot dogs, buns, condiments, salads and drinks. As soon as the cattle were moved, Lee and Tanner had set up a fire pit and started the fire.

"Was a good day, Lee," his second cousin, Keith, said as Lee tossed another log on the fire.

"I think so," Lee returned. "Cattle behaved, no major wrecks." And as he had done most of the day, his eyes sought and found Abby, on the edges of the circle, taking pictures. He wished she would quit and come and sit beside him. He thought she would be done by now.

"It was a tame ride overall," Tanner concurred, sitting beside Keira, his arm draped around her shoulders. "Monty didn't want to take any chances."

"Considering we had a few greenhorns riding with us, I was right." Monty was standing behind Ellen, a cup of coffee in one hand, his other resting on his wife's shoulder as he looked around the gathering. "But I do want to say I'm so thankful for everyone who came out and joined us. This wasn't a full-on cattle drive—Refuge Ranch doesn't run as many cattle as it's capable of—but we're expanding and we hope to bring it back to its full capacity over the next few years."

Lee caught his father staring at him and sensed the question hovering between them.

Then he glanced over at Abby, still hiding behind her camera, and he pushed himself up from the fire. He walked around the gathering to where she was, looking down now at the LCD screen, checking the photo she just took.

"Do you want to catch a shot of the landscape in moonlight?" he asked.

Abby gave him a saucy smile. "Is that cowboy talk for 'do you want to see my etchings?'"

"Those I have back at the ranch," he said, grinning at her humor. "This is exactly what I said it is. The moon is full, but we need to get away from the fire to get the full effect."

"Then I'll come." She lowered her camera, but looped the strap around her neck and picked up her tripod.

Lee tried not to look back as they meandered away from the fire, past the horses who were haltered and tied to a high line. A few nickered at them as they walked past, and Abby stopped, to take a few more photos.

"You're going to have a tough time trying to figure out which of the 2,478 pictures you took to use," Lee teased gently.

"It will be, but once I get the theme of the story, that will narrow down my choices."

"And what is the theme?"

"I don't have it nailed down yet, but it's been coming together the past few days." She gave him a quick smile as they ducked through a scrub of pine trees, then came out into the ridge Lee wanted to show her.

The land spread out below them lit by the watery gleam of the moon, casting eerie shadows.

"See that ridge over to your left?" Lee asked, pointing it out to Abby. "That's where I took you the first time we went out."

"I didn't think we'd ridden that far today," she said as she set up her tripod and attached her camera.

"Dad wanted to make the drive worthwhile, so we chose to go to one of the further pastures today."

She nodded as she looked through the eyepiece. The only sound in the ensuing silence was the now familiar click and whirr of Abby's camera. Lee waited, knowing she would be done on her own time.

"Your father talked about expanding and you mentioned it the other day, as well. How will he manage?" she asked when she was done.

Lee heard the underlying question and paused, looking out over the faintly illuminated landscape. He felt as if he were physically and mentally standing on the edge. His mind flicked back to the first moment he had stopped at the lookout point. How his soul had felt instantly refreshed.

"I'm thinking of staying," he confided. "I want to talk to Dad once all this anniversary stuff is over and see about quitting my job and coming back to the ranch. Working my way into ownership of it, if he'll let me."

"I think that's a good decision." She stepped away from her camera and turned to him. "You belong here. That's not hard to see. This is where you should be. And as for your father, I think he would be thrilled."

He smiled down at her, her eyes dark pools in her pale face, her hair a subdued auburn in the pale light. "I hope so," he said huskily, fingering a strand of hair away from her face.

He wanted to ask her more about what she thought of his decision, but knew this wasn't the time or place. They were still figuring out how things were between them. And although he sensed she had forgiven him for what had happened to her father, he wasn't entirely sure all the barriers had been washed away yet. So, for now, it was enough for her to know that he was staying here. Settling down and making his life on the ranch. It was the first, big step.

Then he took a step of his own, moving in closer to her, letting his hand rest on her shoulder. Their eyes locked and he read the unspoken invitation. Then he lowered his head, pressed his lips to hers and pulled her close.

She responded to him, wrapped her arms around his neck, clinging to him.

After a few moments Lee drew back, dragging in a deep, steadying breath. He kept his arms around her, as if making sure she wasn't leaving.

"So, now what?" Abby whispered, giving voice to one of the questions loitering in his mind.

"I can kiss you again," Lee drawled, anticipation and concern warring with each other at the uncertainty in her voice.

"You could," she said, then reached up on tiptoe and followed through herself. Then she pulled back a ways, looking up at him, a dent of concern between her eyebrows. "But I think we both know there are other things to deal with."

Lee's chest lifted in a weary sigh. "After tonight you're done here." He stated the obvious again, bringing it out into the open. "Where are you going next?"

Abby lowered her gaze, her one hand coming down to rest on his chest. She fingered the flap of his shirt pocket, buying herself a little time. "I've been trying to do some more freelance assignments and I got a line on some promotional work that a hotel chain in Japan wants me to do for them."

"Sounds interesting," Lee said quietly, not sure he liked the sound of that.

"The money is good," she returned. "And it lets me help out my mom a bit."

And there it was again, that specter from the past that would always hang over them.

Dear Lord, how long must I atone for that mistake? Lee prayed.

"So, we'll see. I have to say, however, that I'd love to do more pieces like I'm doing now."

He tilted her chin with his fingertips, bringing her gaze up to his. "You enjoyed this?"

"Oh yes." Her smile gave him some hope. "I loved finding out the story behind the story. The history of this place and the heritage. Interviewing your parents brought it all alive."

"And my charming personality as I showed you around the place," he added, trying to lighten the mood.

"That above all," she said with a grin.

"So, when would you start that job?" he asked, trying not to read too much into what she was saying.

"I haven't taken it yet. I'm still debating."

"Debating what?" he pressed, then wished he would have let that question stay unspoken. He was pushing too hard.

"I have a few things to think about," she said, giving him a wistful look. "If I want to strike out on my own, I'd have to build up my portfolio. Start up a website."

"You must have a bunch of pictures already."

"Actually I do." She sighed. "I just need to figure out if I can make a go of it."

Lee said nothing for a moment, recognizing the reality of Abby's life.

Then a rustling in the trees behind them caught his attention, and he whirled around in time to see Keira breaking through the trees. "Lee? Is that you?" she called out. "Is Abby with you?"

Keira's panicked voice made Lee's heart drop, and when she came closer he saw the tears on her cheeks.

"What's wrong? Is Mom okay? Dad?"

"Yes, they're fine," she said, swiping at her cheeks. "Sorry for being so dramatic, but I need to talk to Abby." Keira looked past Lee, then rushed over to Abby's side, grabbing her by the arms.

"Can you help me out? My wedding photographer, Dana, just called to cancel. Her mother just passed away and she needs to go help out her father. I need someone to take pictures. Would you be able to?"

Abby glanced from Keira to Lee, looking confused.

"Please. I'm so stuck," his sister pleaded. "I don't even know where to start looking on such a short notice."

"But I've never done a wedding before," Abby said, sounding hesitant. "You don't even know what kind of work I do."

"You work for a magazine. I'm sure you're fantastic." Keira swung her gaze toward her brother. "Can you convince her to do it? Please?"

"I think you'd do an amazing job," Lee said, giving Abby an encouraging smile. "Just make sure you hold out for a decent fee."

"Hey, whose side are you on?" Keira protested. But Lee heard the hope in his sister's voice.

"I'm on your side always, sis. But at the same time, I think it would be a great opportunity for you, Abby. Broaden that portfolio you were talking about."

She gave him a hesitant look and then she turned to Keira and nodded. "Okay. I'll take the pictures, but like I warned you, I'm no wedding photographer."

"Thank you, thank you, thank you," she said, grabbing Abby and giving her a tight hug. "You've saved the day for me! Thanks so much." She spun around and started to head back through the woods. "I need to go tell Mom and Tanner. They'll be so relieved."

And as quickly as she had come, she was gone, leaving Lee and Abby alone again.

"Well, that was interesting," Lee said, turning back to Abby, who still looked a bit stunned.

"I'll say." She gave him a small, tentative smile. "Guess you're not rid of me yet."

Lee returned her smile. "Guess not."

He couldn't hide his relief. They had a few more days' grace. A few more days to see what might happen between them.

Keira was a beautiful bride, Abby thought, looking through her camera lens at the young woman dressed in white. Her eyes seemed to glow in anticipation of her wedding which was happening in less than an hour.

"Just move in a little closer," Abby directed, looking up from her camera, now attached to a tripod. She had sat Keira between her brides-maids, Heather and Brooke, on an old log on the edge of the creek. Their long, filmy blue dresses were pulled up around their knees, their bouquets of pink lilies and blue cornflowers resting on their bunched-up dresses. Keira's bouquet was almost identical except the florist had added delphiniums and ivy to hers, filling it out and making it more dramatic. The girls had taken their shoes off as Abby had instructed.

"Okay, now put your feet in the water, okay?" Abby added.

The girls giggled but complied.

"That's going to be a great shot," Lee murmured from his position behind her.

She tried not to pay too much attention to him. He'd been enough of a distraction the entire time she was taking pictures. But with every move she was fully aware of him. Every photo she took of the group, she felt as if he were looking into her camera deep into her heart.

Abby shot off a rapid set of images, then refocused and took a few more. "Now, girls, for the next shot, you have to sit absolutely still, okay? Don't move a muscle."

"My feet are getting cold," Heather complained.

"I promise, it will be worth it," Abby said with a grin and a thumbs-up at the girls.

"I think we're suffering for your art," Keira returned with a grin.

"Prepare to be amazed," Abby joked as she bent over to look through the eyepiece of her camera. The women were laughing and Abby smiled, as well. Shooting this wedding had been a lot more fun than she ever thought. When she was taking photography in school, the instructor had tried to convince her to go in that direction, but she had disdained that advice, saying she wanted to do more serious work that would have an impact on society.

Abby frowned. As if shooting photos of resorts was changing the world…

But the rapport between the bridal-party members was infectious, and Abby pushed her niggling doubts aside. She was genuinely excited to see what the pictures would turn out like. Somehow she could see herself doing this again.

"Why do they have to sit still?" Lee asked.

"I'm slowing down the shutter speed," Abby explained, adjusting the dial on her camera. "That way the moving water will blur and, hopefully, not their feet." She used her remote to trigger the camera, then checked the shot. Perfect. The girls' legs, dresses and bouquets were in clear focus, but the water flowing past their feet was a frothy, foamy blur.

She took a few more images, just to be sure.

"Wow. What a cool effect," Lee said, his admiration giving her a tiny thrill.

Of course, most everything Lee did today gave her that thrill. From the first moment she saw him putting on a suit jacket in the house, tightening his tie and running a brush through his dark brown hair, her heart had been doing these silly little flops. Her feelings for him seemed to intensify every moment they spent together, and she couldn't stop dreaming of kissing him again. "Thanks. Being a wedding photographer is kind of fun."

"Do you enjoy this more than your other work?" he asked.

"Surprisingly I do."

"Well, if that's the case, I believe I heard something about Heather wanting you to do her nuptials too," he said with a grin. "I think you could stay busy here. From what I've seen, you're far better than the photographer Keira initially hired."

Sensing there was more behind his comment than career advice, Abby felt her heart do a slow turn. As if he was feeling her out and trying to find out if she would consider switching her career.

Even before the recent emotional upheaval Lee had created in her life, she knew she had been toying with the idea of change.

"It's a...possibility," Abby said cautiously. She felt as if she and Lee were dancing around the edges of something more. Something deeper. Trying to see what each was willing to do or sacrifice.

"I'd like to think it's more than that," he said.

"Can you two stop with the confab over there and tell us whether or not we can go?" Keira called out, lifting her feet out of the water. "In case you didn't know, I do have a wedding to attend!"

Abby pulled her thoughts back to the job at hand, then put the lens cap on the camera. "Yes, you're free to go. That was the last shot."

Tanner hurried to Keira's side to help her up,

as did the other groomsmen. Lee also crossed the creek on the log bridge to do the same for Brooke.

The girls put their shoes on and they brushed any remnants of leaves off their dresses. Abby was surprised they were game to do this before the wedding, but Keira insisted that once the ceremony was over, she wanted their guests to be able to go directly to the dinner reception, and not have to wait on wedding pictures.

The bridal party climbed into the trucks that brought them here and Abby quickly gathered her equipment together and got into the backseat of the truck Lee drove. They bounced over the fields toward the ranch where a large white tent had been set up. Abby could see people gathering already. She fought down a flutter of panic thinking she should be there already, snapping photos of people as they arrived.

But Keira had clearly stated that once the official wedding pictures were done, she didn't want any of the ceremony. Which gave Abby some breathing space.

The trucks drove to the back of the barns and the bridal party got out.

Abby still could not get over the transformation that had occurred the past few days while she was at her mother's apartment, hunched over her computer, editing the pictures for the magazine article.

A large white tent with three swooping pinnacles dominated one side of the open yard closer to the Bannisters' house. The tent was filled with tables covered with brown cloths and burlap runners. Mason jars filled with white lilies, and big fat sunflowers sat in the center of every table surrounded by smaller glass jars holding floating candles. Large paper lanterns filled the roof of the tent, and each pole was draped with mini lights swathed in tulle.

The chairs that would soon be sitting around the table now were spaced out in equal rows, bordering a carpeted aisle leading to a wooden podium. A large wooden pergola that Abby knew John had been working on for days before framed the podium. Huge bouquets of lilies, sunflowers and cattails filled four cylindrical vases resting in a metal stand, which flanked each post of the pergola. A spray of similar flowers decorated the top of the arch, and cream and brown ribbons twined around its side.

Simple, effective and stunningly beautiful.

Abby was sorry that Keira didn't want any photos of the ceremony. She had said she didn't want the service disrupted, but once it was over, Abby hoped to convince Keira to allow a few by the pergola.

The bridal party exited the trucks and went into one of the barns that had been cleaned out and readied for them to wait until the ceremony started.

"I asked the ushers to save a seat for you toward the front," Lee said, touching her on the shoulder.

Abby jumped, then turned to him, fighting, once again, her reaction to him. He was a handsome man already, but seeing him in a suit and tie, his dark hair gleaming, his face clean-shaven, created a quiver in her midsection.

And when he smiled at her, that quiver became a ripple.

"Thanks for that," she whispered.

People scurried around them, getting ready, touching up makeup, combing hair, giggling, laughing and sharing jokes. She felt as if they were an island in the bustle surrounding them.

"Don't know if I told you, but you look beautiful."

Abby glanced down at the simple rust-colored sheath she had chosen. She wanted to look elegant but unobtrusive at the same time. Her mother had helped her pull her hair back to one side and secure it with a silver clip, letting the rest fall to over her shoulder.

"Thanks," she said, suddenly breathless at his appreciative stare. Then he touched her cheek with one finger. It was the barest of touches. The hint of a caress, but combined with the way his eyes seemed to delve into her soul, it made her all weak in the knees.

"I…I should go," Abby said, her pulse thrumming in her throat.

Lee glanced around, then pulled her into a stall in the barn, slipped his arm around her waist and gave her a gentle, lingering kiss. "I'll see you later," he whispered.

Abby swallowed, his promise making her heart race. Then she nodded, ducked her head and hurried out of the barn. She stepped into the bright sunshine, gave herself a moment to catch her breath, cool her cheeks.

What lay ahead for them?

Chapter Eleven

"I, Tanner Fortier, take you, Keira Bannister, to be my lawfully wedded wife. I promise to stand beside you and support you in sickness and in health. I promise to never leave you or forsake you. I make this promise before God and his people gathered here."

Tanner's voice rang out with conviction in the open air as he stood tall, his hands clasped in Keira's, his dark eyes on hers, and spoke those tender words from his heart. His black suit jacket emphasized his broad shoulders, and the pale blue flowers pinned to his lapel matched the flowers in Keira's bouquet.

The bride looked stunning in a simple, flowing dress trimmed with lace on the hem.

Abby saw Keira's lips tremble as her hands clung to Tanner's. She knew some of the difficulties Tanner and Keira had gone through to get to this point. But now they stood with the mountains on one side of them, a gathering of friends and family on the other side, pledging their love for each other.

They had overcome much; could she and Lee do the same?

Abby's eyes drifted over to Lee. He was watching his sister and Tanner, but then he shifted his gaze and unerringly found hers.

He released a slow, secretive smile that melted her heart.

She cared for him. More than she thought possible. High school all over again.

But as soon as that thought was formulated, she knew they were both well past that simpler time. She and Lee had gone through many valleys to get to where they were now. Spending time with him had shown her a man who had faced his faults and atoned for them. A man who had reconnected with his faith.

Just as she had.

She made herself concentrate on Keira and Tanner. They were exchanging rings and more vows and another heartfelt smile.

"In the name of God the Father, Son and Holy Ghost and by the power invested in me, I now pronounce you husband and wife." Pastor Dykstra's words rang out, a joyful benediction on

Tanner and Keira. Tanner drew his bride tenderly close, gave her a kiss to seal the promise.

Before the people surged to their feet, Abby hurried to the end of the aisle to snap them coming down. People were clapping as music burst forth from the sound system, and Tanner took Keira's hand and together they almost ran down the aisle, Keira's waist-length veil drifting like a gossamer cloud behind her.

The bridesmaids looked like blue butterflies in their flowing dresses as they followed Tanner and Keira down the aisle.

But when Lee and Brooke proceeded down, Abby's hands trembled. He seemed to know, because just before she clicked the shutter, he winked at her. She didn't have a chance to check if she'd captured that.

She took pictures of the receiving line and then commandeered the wedding party again, bringing them to the arch. After that, she took a few more posed pictures, including the one she wanted the most: Tanner's and Keira's hands, wearing their rings, silhouetted against the mountains.

"Are we done?" Tanner asked, obviously eager to get on to the next part of the festivities.

Abby checked the last couple of shots. "Yes. We are."

"I'm so excited to see the pictures," Keira

gushed, giving Abby a thankful smile. "I can't tell you how much I appreciate what you've done for us today."

"It was my pleasure," Abby said. "The setting is amazing and you were all so cooperative. I had a great time."

"As did we all," Lee put in.

Thankfully no one else heard his cheeky comment or noticed the blush warming Abby's cheeks as the bridal party left to freshen up before making their grand entrance into the tent.

"Shouldn't you be going too?" Abby said.

"Just need to ask you a quick question. Are you saving a dance for me?" he asked softly, tracing the line of her neck with his thumb.

"I'll have to see how busy I am," she said, unable to keep the breathless note out of her voice.

"You won't be that busy," he promised. "I have an inside edge with the bride. Foolproof."

"Nothing is foolproof to a sufficiently talented fool," Abby returned, resorting to humor to maintain her equilibrium. Being around Lee all day, so close and yet only able to see him closely through the lens of her camera, had increased her awareness of him.

"Ouch." Lee made a face, pressing a hand to his heart and squishing the flower on his lapel.

"Don't mangle the boutonniere," she chided. "I might need a few more pictures."

"You have tons." He caught her hand and brushed a kiss over her lips. "And that will have to do until I get to dance with you."

Then he sauntered away without looking back to check her reaction to his tender caress.

Abby sucked in a quick breath, then walked back to the tent. Once she was inside, all she could see was a sea of unfamiliar faces.

It was a testament to how well liked the Bannisters were, she thought as she looked around the gathering. The sun was going down and the glowing lanterns, mini lights and candles gave it an air of festive celebration.

Then she saw Monty standing up toward the front of the tent, waving at her. Abby ducked past the rows of tables set out on the grass and made her way across the wooden dance floor made especially for the occasion. Adana, John's daughter, and John's in-laws sat at the table, as did Alice, Tanner's stepmother. Adana sat on Paige Argall's lap, toying with her necklace. The little girl's hair had fallen loose from her floral headpiece and her flushed cheeks and bright eyes showed her weariness.

Abby gave everyone a quick greeting, feeling as if Lee's kiss still lay warm on her lips.

"So, how is it going?" Ellen asked. "I'm hoping for some good family photos to send out with the Christmas cards. We have so much to celebrate this year. So much good news to share."

"I got some good shots." Abby adjusted the settings on her camera for the lighting inside the tent, trying not to feel the weight of the family's expectations for the perfect shot. "I'll know best when I put them up on the computer."

"I can't tell you how happy Keira is that you were able to fill in at the last minute. She was so distraught when the photographer cancelled."

"Glad I could help," Abby said with a gracious smile.

Then the MC told everyone to stand while he announced the entrance of the bridal party. Raucous country music blasted from the speakers as John and Heather, then Lee and Brooke, sashayed into the tent, the girls waving their bouquets. Abby clicked as many photos as she could as Lee and John lifted up their escorts, spun around once and set them in their chair. Then Keira and Tanner came in, looking both radiant and relieved. They didn't repeat their bridal party's antics; instead, Tanner pulled out the chair for Keira, bent over and gave her a sweet kiss.

Everyone sat down and a quiet expectation fell on the crowd.

"I think the food is ready," the MC announced. "We're going to pray and after that please go up and partake in the sumptuous dinner buffet that has been laid out." He flashed a big smile as he looked down from the stage at the wedding guests. "Once we're done eating, I'm going to need a few volunteers to clear the edges of the dance floor so we can move onto that portion of the celebration. But before we start, let's bow our heads, thanking the Lord for this food and for this very special day…"

Abby set her camera down and looked across the table at Monty and Ellen, who were holding hands. Alice, Tanner's mother, sat beside them, smiling across the table at Adana, who had laid her head on Paige's shoulder. This was an eclectic group, she thought, remembering what Lee had told her about Tanner's stepmother and John's in-laws. Their differences. Their struggles.

But here they sat, united by the joy of the union of a new couple. This family was truly a gift, she thought with a start. A true example of Christian love in action.

Her eyes drifted to the head table, latching on to Lee. To her surprise, he was watching her. He gave her a wide grin and she couldn't help return it. As she turned back to her table, she caught Monty watching her with a benign smile on his face as if he knew exactly what was happening between her and his son. She held his gaze, and Monty nodded once, as if giving her his blessing, then lowered his head.

And just before she bowed her own head, she felt a sense of immeasurable peace wash over her.

"And so, dear sister, as you and Tanner start this new journey, I want to wish you a life of happiness and joy. I want to wish you strength in times of weakness and comfort in the hard times and love over all."

Lee lifted his glass, his throat thickening as he thought of all that Keira and Tanner had gone through to get to this day.

During the ceremony, as he watched Tanner and Keira exchange vows, and now as he saw his new brother-in-law lovingly take Keira into his arms, as he saw John and Heather exchange adoring looks in anticipation of their own wedding, he felt a surge of hope for he and Abby.

Granted theirs wasn't the same journey as what his sisters each had to deal with, but he and Abby also had hurdles to overcome, past events to get through. Keira and Tanner, along with John and Heather, had the love and support of a family and a community holding them. He knew he and Abby could count on the same backing to help them through their own difficulties.

And Abby's parents—would you have their support?

The questions nagged at him as he sat down, but though he buried them, he knew they would have to deal with them someway along the journey.

He walked over to his sister and gave her a tight hug, holding her close.

"Love you, girl," he whispered, then pulled back and, as he did when they were kids, tweaked her nose.

Keira gave him a radiant smile. "I hope the same for you someday," she returned. "Abby is a wonderful person. I'm praying things work out for you two."

"Thanks for that, sis, but today is your day." He returned her smile and then offered his congratulations to Tanner, shaking his hand, giving him a manly one-armed hug.

As he sat down, the MC announced the first dance and Tanner and Keira took to the floor. Abby was unobtrusively taking pictures, her flash going off only occasionally.

Lee did the obligatory groomsmen dance with Brooke as Abby took their picture, as well. Then he took his mom for a few turns. Watched as Keira and Tanner cut the huge slab cake they had chosen for their wedding cake. It was decorated with a saddle, the only nod they had made through all the preparations to Tanner's saddle bronc past and Keira's leather work.

Then, finally, the formalities were over and, he presumed, Abby's duties. Lee tried not to rush to her side as the DJ put on some lively country music. Tried to look all cool and in control.

"So, done now?" Lee asked, one hand on the table beside her, the other on his hip.

"I am," she said with a shy look his way. "Keira has asked a couple of friends to take some candid pictures of the reception and told me I was done. I just hope they'll be happy with the results."

He heard an anxious edge to her voice. "From what I've seen, they'll be thrilled. Keira was impressed with how you set up some of the shots. And, let's face it, as long as you pointed the lens in the right direction, I'm sure they'll be great."

"I think I got that part right," she said lightly as she slipped her camera in its bag and then into her backpack.

"So, can I have this next dance?" he asked, hoping he didn't sound as desperate as he felt.

She looked up at him and nodded. "I'd like that," she whispered, smoothing her hand down the folds of her rust-colored dress. When Lee

saw her for the first time wearing the simple
sheath, her hair pulled back to one side with a
silver clip, falling in a cascade of curls over her
shoulder, he felt as if his breath had been pulled
out of him. She looked stunning.

He took her hand and led her to the wooden
dance floor that he and his father had spent an
entire afternoon putting together. The whole
time he'd been nailing down the sheets of ply-
wood, he imagined himself twirling Abby
around on it.

And now it was a reality.

He took her hand in his, and they quickly
caught the rhythm of the bouncy, country song.
She was light on her feet, graceful and easily
matched his steps.

"You're a good dancer," she said as he spun
her around.

"You are too."

"You're just saying that because I did." She
grinned up at him, ducked under his arm, added
a quick twirl and stepped back into his embrace.

"Getting fancy on me now."

"Practicing for my audition on *Dancing with
the Stars*," she quipped, making another quick
turn.

"And they would be lucky to have you."

She laughed as they worked their way around
the floor, avoiding the other couples. People

were talking and laughing and a party atmosphere had invaded the tent. His father had gotten hold of his phone and, ignoring Lee's and
Abby's protests, had snapped a quick picture
of the two of them. Not that Lee had much to
protest. The idea that they were captured as a
couple seemed to make it more real.

Then the song faded away, the lights dimmed
and the gentle strains of a waltz filled the night.

Lee pulled Abby close and tucked her hand
against his chest, and as she settled into his embrace, he felt his breath leave him in a gentle
sigh. This felt right, he thought, swaying slowly,
his head bent over hers, her arm around his
neck, her other around his waist.

He felt her chest lift and she exhaled softly.

"You okay?" he asked.

"I'm perfect," she said, resting her head on
his chest. "Absolutely perfect."

They made a few more turns around the floor
and he felt as if his life was coming to a good
place. The last time he'd felt this way was the
last time he was with Abby.

Before he went to prison.

"Hey, you," he murmured, pulling back. "Can
we go somewhere private?"

She shot him a wide-eyed look, then slowly
nodded. "Sure. Of course."

He took her hand and made his way through

the people still circling the dance floor. When they passed his parents, he ignored his mother's knowing smile, his father's grin.

The moon was no longer full, but it was still light enough to make his way across the yard, away from the music and noise of the wedding tent.

"So, where are you taking me?" she asked, nervous laughter edging her voice.

"Right here," he said, stopping at a pile of square bales he and John had set up for some of the photos Abby had requested. The bales were stacked two down, one up for a backrest and draped with cloth. He settled down on the lower one, leaning against the one behind, and held out his hand for Abby. She didn't seem to need another invitation and sat down beside him, resting her head on his shoulder. She fit perfectly in his embrace.

In the corrals beyond, the horses whinnied softly, sensing their presence.

"How is our baby calf?" Abby asked, her voice a murmur in the night.

"Doing great. He'll be pail-feeding soon."

"How do you do that?"

Lee gently tucked a wisp of her hair around her ear and smiled. "Abby, I didn't take you out here to discuss the care and feeding of calves."

"So, what *did* you want to talk about?"

"Are you being coy with me?" he asked, resting his chin on her silky hair.

"Who, *me?*"

He smiled, pulling her closer, took a breath and decided to go for broke. "Dad and I are going into town next week to sign me up as partner in the ranch. I'm going to make it official."

"That's great," Abby said, drawing back, but keeping her hands on his chest. "As I mentioned before, I think that's the right thing to do."

He looked down at her, thinking of the conversation they'd had at the cattle drive. About her finding other work. He wasn't sure what to expect of her, but one thing he did know. He wasn't going to let her leave on him again.

"I know that we have a few issues to settle yet," he said, tracing her features with his finger, then pressing a kiss to her lips. "And I know I can't make any assumptions, but I want to think that there's an us. A future."

Abby was quiet and his heart lodged in his throat.

Then she looked up at him and smiled. "I'd like to think so too."

He felt they were still edging around what he wanted to say, but at the same time, other shadows hung over them.

"But there is one thing I need to do before anything can be settled between us," he said softly.

He caught a flare of panic in her eyes.

"I need to talk to your parents. Especially your father. I need to ask their forgiveness."

Abby's hand clung to his, her fingers like a vise. "So soon?"

"The sooner the better. I sense that you're uneasy about it?"

Abby looked down at their joined hands, the moonlight casing her features in shadow. Lee couldn't read her expression. He wanted to tip her face up so he could see, but instead he waited.

"When my folks split up, my father was a broken and hurting man with a lot of problems," she said. "I've struggled with my own difficulties with him, but he has been calling my mom more often the past few weeks. I think he wants to come for a visit. He says he's a different man—that he's turned over a new leaf—so we'll see." She gave him a gentle smile. "Maybe he's different enough from who he was before. Maybe he'll accept what you have to say."

"Then I'll pray that's the case," Lee said.

She looked up at him, her gaze intent, as if she needed to impress whatever she was about to say on him. "You need to know, though, that whatever happens with my father, I hope we can find a way through all this. You matter more to me than anyone I've ever met."

"And you to me," he said, conviction ringing in his voice as the uncertainty, lingering all night, shifted into surety.

He kissed her again and as she settled against him, he looked out over the fields illuminated by the pale light of the moon. Fields that, Lord willing, would soon also be his.

His and Abby's.

Still humming the song that the band played last, Abby made the final turn onto her mother's street. Her lips still felt warm from Lee's kiss. She could still feel his arms around her, still feel herself twirling around the dance floor with her hand in his.

She thought of the pictures she had taken. Heather had approached her at the reception and mentioned that she might like to hire Abby for her own wedding. Assuming Abby would stick around, that is.

She could do more freelance work, as Lee had always hinted at. Make work of getting more local business.

Dreams and plans swirled through her mind, and hovering over all of them was Lee's presence.

And what would your mother think of these new developments?

The thought was like a douse of cold water. Abby wanted to dismiss the question, but she knew Ivy would not so easily be ignored.

At the same time, the words of the pastor's sermon on Sunday had percolated through the events of the week, reminding her that though Lee had made mistakes, so had she. That his sincere apologies were enough. She wanted to move on.

She smiled and then, to her surprise, felt the prickle of tears threatening. Tears of joy and happiness.

Thank you, Lord, she prayed as she slowed down in front of her mother's apartment.

Then stopped. An old pickup was parked in the spot she usually parked in, and there was no room for her vehicle. She spun the wheel, made a quick U-turn to park on the other side of the street. But it was a busy night in the neighborhood and she had to drive to the end of the block before she found a spot to squeeze her car in.

A shiver danced down her spine as she walked down the quiet street, her high heels clacking on the sidewalk. Tonight life was good, she thought with a quick prayer of thanks, wrapping her shawl around her. And for the first time in years, she felt an anticipation that it might get even better.

She crossed over the street, then slowed as a

light flickered on in the old truck parked in front of her mother's apartment. The door opened and her heart jumped into overdrive as a tall, slender figure stepped out. He wore a ball cap that cast his face in shadow from the overhead street-lights, but she could see that he wore a denim jacket, worn blue jeans and work boots.

And in one hand he held a long stick that rested on the ground.

She sent a panicked glance around the deserted street. A single light shone from the upstairs of one of the house, but the rest were dark. No one was around. She was on her own.

She should have accepted Lee's offer to take her home.

Dear Lord, protect me, she thought as she came to a stop, looking for an exit, her heart pounding. Which way to go? Could she outrun him?

"Abby, it's okay," the man called out, his raspy voice achingly familiar. "Abby, it's me—your father."

Abby stopped, her one hand still grasping her camera bag, the other her shawl, as shivers wracked her body.

"Dad?" she returned, taking a slow, cautious step toward him. "Dad…is that you?"

In answer, he pulled his cap off. She could see the glint of his glasses, the brush of a mustache that he'd had as long as she could remember. What she had thought was a stick was only the cane that he started using after the accident.

It really was him.

Then, in spite of everything that had happened, in spite of the sorrow and grief at her parents' divorce, a tiny sob caught in her throat and she hurried her steps. She stopped in front of him, her one hand coming up to touch his dearly familiar face. Still wary, she took a careful sniff and her heart sang.

He didn't smell like alcohol or tobacco.

"Oh, Daddy," she said, her throat thick with emotion as she gave him a tight hug. "I haven't seen you in so long."

"I know, honey. I'm sorry," Cornell murmured into her hair. Then he pulled away, his smile tentative. "I've been trying to contact your mother to arrange a meeting. She wouldn't make a decision, so I took a chance and came anyway."

"Have you been up to the apartment yet?"

He shook his head. "No. But I heard from Louisa that you were at a wedding at the Bannister place, so I thought I would wait until you were home."

"Where did you see Louisa?"

"At the Grill and Chill. She was sitting with that Bamford guy."

Brooke wouldn't be happy to hear that, Abby thought. She brushed the inconsequential thought aside as she tucked her arm into her father's. "How are you feeling? How are things with you?"

He cleared his throat. "I've cleaned up my life, honey. I've made changes too."

"I can see some of them," she said. Then she gave him another tight hug. She pulled back and, to her surprise, saw the glint of tears in his eyes.

"I've missed you," he said hoarsely.

"I've missed you too," she returned. "Come up to the apartment. Let's talk there." The air was still warm, but Abby didn't want to have her reunion with her father take place on a street outside her mother's apartment.

But he shook his head. "Sorry, sweetheart. I don't think your mom wants me up there. And I can't take it if she pushes me away."

Abby bit her lip, thinking, understanding his dilemma. Trouble was, nothing was open this time of night in Saddlebank.

"Come sit inside my truck," he said. "I have a thermos of hot chocolate. I just want to talk."

Abby looked up at her mother's apartment window, but it was dark.

"Please, honey. Just talk. And for you, especially now, because of your relationship with Lee Bannister, it's important."

His enigmatic comment intrigued her and, at the same time, created a shiver of apprehension. "How do you know about my relationship with Lee?"

"Your mom mentioned it. Said that she didn't like it. Then I asked Louisa and she said that you two had been spending a lot of time together. That you were with him at this wedding. That you were thinking of sticking around because of him, but also that you had some…reservations."

Louisa talked too much, Abby thought indignantly.

"Please, come into the truck. I feel like a stalker talking to you out here," Cornell said, walking around the front of his vehicle and opening the passenger door for her. His limp was still pronounced and Abby felt another surge of guilt at her relationship with Lee.

She pushed that down, thinking of her conviction that she and Lee would find a way through all this mess with her father. She couldn't let that waver. Not now.

Inside the truck her father poured some steaming hot chocolate from a thermos into a cup.

"I don't know an easy way to start with this," he said, handing her the cup. "I guess the best place to start is that you need to know that I'm sorry for everything I put you, your mother and your brother through since the accident."

"I'm glad to know that." Abby had lifted the cup to her lips, but before she took a drink she took a sniff. Just to be on the safe side. But all she smelled was chocolate.

"I know my drinking caused a lot of trouble. But…I had lots on my mind," he said.

"Of course. The accident created a lot of difficulty."

Her father nodded, taking a sip from his cup, staring ahead, as if remembering. "So. You and Lee. Is it serious?"

Abby shrugged, her hands wrapped around her cup. "I like him. A lot. I know that might be difficult for you to hear, Dad, but he's very sorry for what he did. He wants to meet you to apologize."

He was quiet so long, Abby's heart clenched. Would this be a problem?

"There's nothing to forgive," he said, his voice quiet. Subdued.

"What do you mean there's nothing to forgive?" Abby lowered her cup, staring at him. "There's everything to forgive. The accident. The repercussions—"

Her father waved off her last statement. "Doesn't matter. All you need to know is that he's a good man. I want you to know that whatever happens, I want to give you both my blessing."

Abby was puzzled by her father's quick assertion and blessing. Though part of her was happy he was able to forgive Lee, she couldn't quash a feeling that something didn't add up. Not after everything her father had always said about Lee. How angry he had been.

"Lee wants to talk to you about your blessing," she said, looking over at her father, concern battling with confusion over his puzzling about-face.

"I don't want to talk to him."

"I understand that," Abby said, reaching out and touching her father's arm, her puzzlement turning into fear. "Of course it will be hard, but it will help him a lot," she urged.

Her father tossed back the last of his hot chocolate. "You just tell him that I'm okay with you and him dating. I'm not going to stand in your way."

"So why can't you tell him yourself?"

"I can't. It's too hard. It's…wrong. All wrong. He didn't…he's not…" Her father waved his hand as if dismissing what Abby wanted.

A curious tone in her father's voice puzzled her. "What do you mean, he didn't. Didn't what?"

Cornell shook his head. "Ignore what I said."

Abby felt a shiver of dread. "Why do I get the feeling there's something you're not telling me?"

"I'm telling you only what you need to know." Her father slammed his cup down and turned toward her, his face contorted with fear.

Abby pulled back, afraid herself at her father's expression. "What do you mean?"

"I can't tell you, Abby. I just can't. There's too much at stake."

"What can't you tell me?" she insisted. "What is going on?"

"It's enough for you to know that Lee is a good guy. That's all I wanted to tell you. I want you to have a happy life."

Something didn't add up and Abby couldn't put her finger on it. "Why are you defending him so vigorously? There was a time when you were just as adamant that he was a horrible, evil young man."

"I was overreacting. He's...not guilty...I mean...he's okay... He's not bad."

But Abby latched on to the one thing her father said that perplexed her more than anything. "That's the second time you've said he's not guilty. What is he not guilty of?"

"Stop it," Cornell hissed. "I can't give the money back. Not anymore. You should never have pushed me to take it. I shouldn't have listened to you. The Bannisters can't find out..."

The air in the cab was suddenly cold. Ominous. "Can't find out what?"

Her father twisted his hands around the steering wheel, growing more agitated.

"Can't find out *what*, Dad? Tell me. What can't the Bannisters find out?"

Her father spun on her, his eyes wide. "That Lee wasn't driving the night of my accident. The wrong person went to jail."

Chapter Twelve

"What do you mean, Lee wasn't driving?" What her father said didn't make any sense. Abby felt as if she were tumbling down a hill, trying to figure out which way was up. "I don't understand. It was his truck. You saw him. The police saw him."

"I shouldn't have said anything. Forget I ever said it." Her father sounded panic-stricken.

"I can't, Dad. You have to tell me what you meant." Abby spoke each word slowly, precisely, as her mind tried to sort through what he had just thrown at her.

Cornell looked away from her, his hands resting on the steering wheel now, kneading it. "Just leave it alone, Abby."

"No. I won't. Tell me what you meant."

He sighed, looking down; then, as if realizing

she wasn't going to let it go, he began talking. Quietly, slowly at first, then gaining momentum.

"Right after I got hit by Lee's truck, I was conscious. I remember seeing the truck hit a tree and the lights of the truck were shining on the branches. I could see two silhouettes in the truck. Then the light inside the truck went on and I saw for sure. Two people. The driver got out, pulled the passenger over and put the seat belt on him."

"Are you sure? Could you have been hallucinating? You were in a lot of pain." Part of Abby wanted desperately to believe her father that it hadn't been Lee who was driving, but another part didn't dare. Believing what he said changed everything.

"I was fairly lucid in spite of the pain," her father continued. "I saw the guy who was driving walk toward me. I couldn't see his face. It was dark and the truck's lights kind of threw him in shadow, but I could see he had long hair. Blond hair. Then he backed off and ran off into the woods."

"How long was his hair? Shoulder length? Curly? Are you sure it was blond? Are you sure you didn't recognize him?" The questions were automatic. The questions of a reporter trying to investigate the story, trying to piece it together. "Did you know who it was?"

Blond, long hair. Driving with Lee. Could it have been Mitch? David? Because if her father was describing the driver accurately, and if his memory was indeed correct, this man definitely wasn't Lee with the close-cropped dark hair he had favored back then.

"No. I had no idea who he was. I just remember seeing him move the passenger, come walking over to me, then run away. I blacked out after that." He scrubbed a hand down his face and sighed wearily. "When I came to in the hospital the police told me Lee was the one driving. I couldn't figure out what was going on. Then a lawyer came and started talking about pressing charges. Suing him. Getting some money. So…I just let events go the way they seemed to be going."

"Why did you do that?"

Cornell stared ahead, his breathing shallow and quick, as if he had run a long ways. "According to the lawyer, the police had Lee behind the wheel and I knew his parents had lots of money. I wanted to ask more—about who else might have been in the truck with Lee— but I had no clue who the other guy was. And I knew if I started asking questions, it would raise inquiries about who was driving, and if that happened…" He let the sentence trail off, but Abby finished it herself.

"We wouldn't have known who to sue," she said, her voice like ice.

She felt her throat close off, her stomach turn over. Lee was innocent. The man she had struggled to forgive had done nothing that required her forgiveness.

Her entire worldview of the past few years was turned upside down, like a toy box being dumped. Everything was scattered on the floor, a clutter of misconceptions and false righteous anger.

Lee had gone to prison for nothing.

"Is this the truth, Daddy?" she croaked.

He slowly nodded and she could see from the shame on his face that he wasn't lying. "You know, I thought the money would make a difference. But it didn't. I lost everything after I got that money. I thought it would help, but it was blood money. Shouldn't have taken it."

Abby's lips were quivering the entire time her father talked. They were cold and numb, just like the rest of her body. She couldn't get warm enough. *Lee wasn't the one who hurt my father. Lee wasn't driving.*

The thought shivered through her, and as the repercussions of her father's reluctant confession became clear, she felt as if the ground were cut beneath her feet. All this time. All these years, her bitterness toward Lee had festered and grown. She had come here as the injured party. Feeling all magnanimous when she decided she could forgive him for what he had done to her father. She felt as if she had overcome a huge hurdle.

But it was all a lie. Everything was the other way around.

Now Lee had to be the one to forgive her.

"You have to promise me one thing, though," her father said, clutching her hand in a fierce grip. "You can't tell him. You can't let him know what you know. I didn't come to tell you this. To confess. I only wanted to let you know that Lee was a good guy. That I wanted to see you with him. I don't want you to waste your life. That's all."

"Lee needs to know," Abby said, the burden of what her father just told her lying like a rock on her chest.

"Please, I'm begging you. Don't tell him. If he knows, his family will want the money back. I don't have it. Your mother doesn't have it. We can't afford to pay them back. I didn't mean to tell you. You kept pushing and pushing—"

Abby shook off her father's hand as a sob clawed to the back of her throat. Panic grabbed her heart with a harsh, unyielding fist.

"I gotta go," she said, the walls of the truck closing in on her. "I've gotta leave."

"Promise me you won't tell him," her father pleaded as she scrabbled at the handle of the door, trying to pull it open. "Promise me you won't tell his family."

Abby finally unlatched the door and clambered out, her feet almost slipping out from her when her heels hit the pavement. She grabbed her camera bag and without another word to her father, scurried down the sidewalk and up the stairs to her mother's apartment.

Minutes later she was inside. She leaned against the door, her legs trembling, her stomach heaving as her father's shattering words circled her brain like threatening crows.

Why now? Why did this happen now?

A cry of anguish choked off her throat as images flooded her mind. Lee asking her forgiveness. The note of self-condemnation in his voice as he spoke of wanting to talk to her father.

She'd been so smug. So self-righteous.

Lee had gone to jail for something that wasn't his fault.

His family had paid out money they never had to.

Abby slid down the door, grabbing her head as if to contain her raging thoughts. She had struggled so hard to forgive him for what she thought he had done to her father. Yes, her life had been difficult, but she hadn't lost her freedom for three years.

As Lee had.

Maybe it was a good thing you ended up in jail.

Guilt seized her midsection. How could she have said that? How could she have thought that?

Lee had spent three years of his life in prison because of her father's mistake and years away from his home, struggling to repay his family because he was so ashamed of what he had done. And now? What would happen now? What would Lee think of her now? How would he react?

The unanswerable questions swarmed through her mind, taunting her. She had been so wrong about Lee in so many ways. He hadn't asked her out on a bet as Mitch and David had told her, and now he hadn't been the one who had injured her father.

She waited a moment, trying to find a solid place, trying to find her footing in this new reality.

You can't tell him.

Abby shook her head, unable to process that thought. How could her father not think Lee needed to know? She had to tell him.

And what would he think then? What would happen between them? Would he have as difficult a time forgiving her as she had forgiving him?

"Abby? Is that you?"

Her mother's voice drifted down the hall. She hurriedly stood, smoothed down her hair, the awful knowledge her father had just given her dragging her down.

"I'm here," Abby said, hitting the light switch for the main room.

We can't afford to pay him back.

The reality of what her father said was made even clearer as she looked around her mother's apartment.

But how could she not tell Lee? The guilt of what he had done had been such a burden on his shoulders.

Abby felt bile rise in her throat. Three years of his life and all that money. Gone. For nothing.

"Abby, honey, are you okay?" Her mother was tying up her bathrobe as she came into the living room.

Did her mother know the truth?

"I'm not okay," she gasped.

"I can see that. Did you get sick at the wedding?"

Oh, dear Lord, the wedding. That moment

of utter bliss and contentment. Happiness and anticipation.

What would Lee think of her and her family after she told him?

Couldn't she just keep it quiet? Keep it to herself as her father suggested?

"No. I didn't get sick." Abby squeezed the heel of her hand to her temple, trying to push away the headache that threatened. "But…I saw Dad."

"Today? When? I thought you were at the wedding."

"I saw him just now. He said he wanted to talk to me." Abby's stomach did another dive as she thought of the topic of that conversation.

"What about?"

"Lee." Abby set her backpack with her camera on the dining table and turned to her mother. "Did you know about the accident? I mean, did you know the truth about the accident? Did Dad ever talk about it?"

Her mother's puzzled frown gave her some encouragement that maybe she didn't know. "What truth about the accident?"

Abby folded her arms over her stomach as she leaned back against the table for support. "Dad just told me… He just said…Lee wasn't the one who was driving when he got hit. Someone else was."

"What are you saying? I don't understand."

Abby eased out a sigh. Then, in a dull monotone, she relayed to her mother what she had heard from her father. "And, on top of that, he told me not to tell Lee," she said.

Ivy pressed her fingers to her lips, her shell-shocked gaze darting around the apartment, as if mentally sizing it up just as Abby had done only a few moments ago. "If you tell Lee…the money…we were wrong…I can't pay that kind of money back."

"I know. Neither can Dad. It's gone."

"And the Bannisters could sue us. For libel. Or something. Your father could be charged."

Her mother's despair created a storm of second thoughts. Lee seemed content. He had made his peace with what happened. He had found his way through all this. Nothing could be changed by his knowing.

"Are you going to tell him?" her mother asked, her voice shrill.

"I have to," Abby said quietly. "It's not fair."

"But if he finds out what will he do?"

"I don't know."

And that was the truth.

"I'm tired, Mom. I need to go to bed. We'll talk about this tomorrow." She gave Ivy a quick kiss, then grabbed her purse and trudged to her room, worry and fear and anger with her father dogging her steps. Why had her father lied and, even worse, kept up the deception all these years?

That wasn't hard to figure out, she realized as she closed the door and tugged her shoes off. He saw a chance to get some money and he took it.

And Abby had been right beside him, urging him on, her own rage with Lee entwined in with what she saw as a gross injustice done to her father.

Instead, it was the other way around and she had been a party to it.

Help me, Lord, she prayed, dropping her head into her hands, squeezing her eyes shut as if trying to hold back the emotions that threatened to swamp her. *Help me.*

She was so confused she didn't even know what to ask of God anymore.

She lifted her head and saw her Bible sitting beside her laptop. She dragged it across the desk, opening it to Lamentations 3, a passage that she had read over and over again after her father's accident.

Because of the Lord's great love, we are not consumed, for his compassions never fail. They are new every morning; great is your faithfulness.

She would require more of the Lord's faithfulness in the coming days. Because one thing was certain, as hard as it had been for her to forgive Lee, he had much more to forgive. She had pushed the lawyer so hard to fight for what she thought of as a reasonable settlement. And now, looking back, she knew her motives weren't exactly pure. Some of her insistence had to do with the "bet" that she thought Mitch and David had made with Lee. She had thought if she could get back at him she would feel better.

But it hadn't done anything for her. And now not only had her father lied, but her own twisted motives had saddled Lee with a financial burden that, by his own admission, had been part of the reason he stayed away from the ranch.

What if she didn't tell him the truth? Wouldn't it be easier?

Abby shook that thought off even while it was formulating. She couldn't do that. Lee carried the burden of guilt so heavily. She needed to release him from the lie that hung over his head with the truth.

But what would he do? How would he react?

How could he forgive her father and, by extension, her?

Lee pulled up to the Grill and Chill, curiosity and expectation thrumming through him. Abby hadn't been in church this morning. Though he and his family had been up until 3:00 a.m.

cleaning up after the wedding, he still got up to get to Sunday services on time, looking forward to seeing her. When she didn't show up, he thought she was having second thoughts. But her text, asking him to meet at the Grill and Chill afterward, balanced out the concerns.

He stepped inside the café and glanced around.

George Bamford was standing at the till, dealing with a customer.

"Hey, Bannister," the man said, giving him a cursory nod as he closed the drawer of the antique cash register. "So. Wedding went good?"

"It was great. Lots of fun. Brooke looked gorgeous. Too bad you couldn't have come." Lee had heard via Keira that Brooke had asked George to come with her as her escort, but he hadn't shown.

"Allison was at the wedding too. One of us had to stay back and keep the grill going," George said, glowering at Lee as if it were his entire fault he couldn't attend.

"Well, maybe next time…" Lee said.

"Next time being yours?" George asked slyly, looking over his shoulder to the back of the restaurant, where Lee saw Abby sitting.

"No. Heather's, for now," Lee countered, then added a quick lift of his eyebrow as if letting the other man know that there might be another one in the future.

"Go get 'em, cowboy," George said. "I'll be by with coffee."

Lee grinned, then headed to the booth at the end, where Abby sat, looking down at the coffee in front of her as if it held the secrets of the universe.

"Hey, you," he said, slipping into the booth. He wanted to kiss her but figured he'd hold off. Plenty of time for that later.

She simply looked up at him. Lee couldn't stop a twitch of concern at the haggard look on her face.

"You okay?" he asked, reaching over and laying the back of his hand against her cheek. "You look exhausted."

She didn't reply, but she reached up and caught his hand, holding it against her face, her slender fingers curled around his wrist. Then she lowered her hand, still holding his, her fingers like ice.

"What's wrong, Abby?"

She gave him a smile, but Lee could see her heart wasn't in it. George came by with a pot of coffee. She declined a refill, but Lee nodded at George. When he left she pushed her cup aside, sitting back in the booth, her arms clasping her middle, and Lee had a nagging suspicion that she was about to tell him something he didn't want to hear.

"I saw my dad last night," she said, her voice so quiet he had to lean forward to hear her. "He was parked in front of my mom's apartment. I saw him when I came back from…from the wedding." She stopped there, teeth worrying her lower lip, her eyes still averted.

"How is he?" Lee asked, his heart faltering. Had seeing her father given her second thoughts?

"He's okay. He came to give me his blessing. On our relationship."

Lee felt his breath leave him like air out of a balloon. "That's great. That's good to know."

However, Abby didn't look as happy as he felt. "But while we were talking, I found something else out. Something important." She bit her lip again, then looked up at him, her eyes brimming with tears. "My dad told me that you weren't the one driving when he got hit. That there was another person in the truck when it hit you and he was the one driving. He was the one who hit my dad. Not you."

Lee narrowed his eyes, trying to keep up. "I don't understand what you're saying," he said, truly bewildered as he tried to process what she was saying. "I was the only person in the truck when Sheriff McCauley came by. Just me."

"According to my father, after he was hit, he saw the truck hit the tree. That's when he saw two people in the cab. He said he saw the driver get out and pull the passenger—you—over to the driver's side. Then the driver ran over to my father." A deep frown creased her brow, but she pushed on. "My dad couldn't see who it was, but he could see that it was a guy with blond hair, kind of long. Obviously not you. But he couldn't see his face. Then whoever it was ran off into the bushes and minutes later the police were there."

"There were two people in my truck?" Lee repeated, trying to make sense of what Abby was telling him. "And your dad is actually saying I wasn't driving when I hit him?"

"Yes, that's what he said. You don't remember any of this?"

"The last thing I remember was walking with Mitch and David to my truck after the party." Lee stared at Abby. "Is he absolutely sure about all this?"

"I had to drag the truth from him, but yes," she whispered. "He was quite sure."

Lee fell back against the seat, feeling as if he'd been punched in the gut. Too vividly he remembered sitting with his father at the lawyer's office across from Abby, her mother and

Cornell's attorney while they laid out the terms of the settlement.

It was the lowest point in his life. Not only finding out what he had done, but realizing that his father would be paying for his mistake as well when the insurance company refused to pay up because this was Lee's third DUI. But the worst was seeing Abby glaring at him as if he was even less worthy than scum.

And what about now?

"Did you know this all along?"

"No. No, I didn't," Abby said, shaking her head vehemently. "Like I said, I had to drag the truth out of my dad. He made some vague comments and when I pushed him he finally told me. I had no clue. No earthly idea."

"I spent three years in jail," he snapped, his brain scrambling to absorb what Abby had just told him. "Three years of my life thinking I was nothing but dirt. And then another three years trying to pay my dad back."

"I'm so sorry," Abby said. "So sorry. I should never have pushed my dad to ask for a settlement."

"You were the one who wanted to sue?"

"I encouraged him to," she whispered brokenly. "I'm so sorry."

"Sorry?" Lee shook his head, his confusion morphing into an irrational anger. "You're *sorry.*

I spent years paying my father back the money you pushed your father to sue for. Money that your father squandered."

He stopped himself, though the stricken look on Abby's face made him realize he couldn't take back what he said.

But he didn't have room for her right now. All he could think about was what she and her father did to him. The guilt that had dogged him. The look of disgust on her face when they had faced each other across the lawyer's table as they hammered out a deal. The money they had sucked out of his parents.

"I gotta go," he muttered, grabbing his hat, slipping out of the booth.

Then he turned and strode out of the diner, shoved open the door and walked blindly to his truck. He got in, twisted the key in the ignition, then pulled out of the parking spot, his tires squealing, his foot pressed to the accelerator.

He had to get out of here. He couldn't be here right now.

Chapter Thirteen

Abby sat back in the booth, her eyes stinging with tears, her heart heavy as a stone as she watched Lee stride away from her, each footfall like a hammer blow to her chest.

She leaned her elbows on the table, pressing the heels of her hands into her eyes, willing back the tears that even now spilled past her hands and down her cheeks.

Be with him, Lord, she prayed. *Keep him safe.*

She wanted to pray that he could forgive her, but she remembered how angry she had been with him over what she thought he had done to her father. It had taken her years to get to the point that she could forgive him.

How long would it take him?

She blindly fished in her backpack for a tissue. She wiped her eyes, but new tears flowed down her scalding cheeks. It didn't matter how long it would take Lee to forgive. She guessed that anything they had before had been destroyed in the aftermath of this particular storm.

She pulled a few bills out of her wallet and dropped them on the table. Then she struggled to her feet, grabbing her backpack, and made her way out of the café, hoping no one would notice her streaked makeup, her red eyes.

She wasn't sure how she made it back home. Her mother was waiting for her with a pot of tea, but Abby declined, retreating to her bedroom.

She dropped into her chair and turned on her laptop. She had spent the entire weekend editing pictures and writing up the article for the magazine. She had gone over it so many times, trying to catch the right nuances, give it the right due.

But the hardest part of all was seeing the pictures of Lee.

And there were so many of them: Lee on a horse. Lee with their dog, Sugar. Lee with the calf. Lee standing on a hill overlooking a valley. Lee smiling at her, his eyes twinkling.

Each picture hurt to look at. Each picture a reminder of what might have been.

And now she had the wedding photos to go through, as well.

She loaded them onto her computer, hoping, praying she could be dispassionate about them as she sorted through them all, discarding and narrowing the choices to her top picks.

She pulled up the last pictures she had edited and felt, again, that clench in her heart as Lee's smiling face stared back at her.

So close, she thought, her heart aching. They had come so close.

All the while, as she edited the wedding photos—softening, shading, adding highlights, enchanting and vignetting—Abby kept her phone beside her. She had tried to call him a few times, but he didn't answer and she didn't blame him.

What could they possibly have to say to each other now?

But each time she saw Lee's smiling face, it was like another bruise on her battered soul. She had been wrong about him twice. She wasn't worthy of him.

Not anymore.

"So let me get this straight, you weren't the one driving when your truck hit Cornell Newton?"

Monty sat back in the leather chair of his office, his incredulous look echoing the anger that had twisted Lee's gut when Abby told him.

"According to Cornell, there was another driver," Lee said, turning to look out the window over the ranch he would become a part of.

"He didn't know who, but from the description, I'd guess David. He's the last person I remember being with that night." Lee pinched the bridge of his nose, his brain still reeling from the information Abby had dumped on him an hour ago. "I don't know what to do. What to think."

He heard the squeak of his father's chair and then a hand resting on his shoulder. "This is hard news, son. Very hard news."

"I keep thinking of how guilty I felt. When I saw Abby at the lookout point when I first came back home, she was so angry with me and I felt I deserved every bit of it. But now…?"

He closed his eyes and rested his forehead against the window, thinking of the furious words he had thrown at her in the café. The guilt on her face. It destroyed him and at the same time he felt suddenly exonerated. He had thought himself worthless for so long. Unworthy of Abby. When she had accepted his apology, granted him forgiveness, he felt as if all the self-condemnation he had put himself through was eased away.

But all those emotions were for nothing. Everything was different now.

"Now you have to find a way through all this," his father said. "A way to redeem this."

Lee whirled around. "How? I lost three years of my life because of a lie. Abby's father took that away from me. And the lawsuit…the lawsuit Abby admitted to pushing her father to file…that took another five to pay you back. It set the ranch back for a number of years." He spoke the words through gritted teeth, his hands clenched at his sides. "How am I supposed to get around that? My reputation was ruined for a crime I didn't commit. I wasted all that time and money trying to make up for what I'd done. All those years. Gone. Lost."

Monty gave him a sympathetic smile, then leaned back against the desk, looking contemplative. "Maybe. But I remember hearing a sermon once on that very topic. The fact that nothing in our life is wasted. That God uses everything that comes our way."

"Well, at least you got most of your money back," Lee said with a harsh laugh. "I'm thankful for that."

"You know I never asked for you to repay me," Monty said quietly, his arms folded over his barrel chest.

"I know, but I owed you for what I'd put you through. You had to sell all those cows, borrow money against the ranch even though it was paid off. Now, turns out, I didn't put you through anything. Cornell and Abby did."

"Don't blame Abby," Monty chided. "At the

time she was only trying to find a way to make up for what happened to her father."

"I know that on one level, but it's hard not to feel humiliated at how I practically begged for her forgiveness when it turns out I didn't do anything to merit it." He could still feel the sting of it all. Especially given the frosty welcome he'd received when he first came back to Saddlebank.

His father pursed his lips, tapping his fingers on his arm as if considering something.

"You've got your thinking face on," Lee said, dropping his hands on his hips. "What's on your mind, Dad?"

Monty was quiet for another moment, and then he gave Lee a pensive look. "I'm thinking of Mitch and David. They were bad men. Evil, you could say, given what they did to your sisters."

"Not hard to agree with that," Lee said, wondering where his father was going with this dark history when they were talking about what Cornell had done.

"But you were friends with them."

"In high school," Lee protested. "And for a few months afterward." Surely his father didn't hold him accountable for Mitch and David's actions?

"The accident happened after a party you

attended with those friends," Monty continued. "You were drinking with those friends."

"But I wasn't driving."

"I know—I understand that—but let's work this through." Monty paused, then gave Lee a melancholy smile. "I can't begin to tell you how sad I am that you were falsely charged. And I'm also very sorry that this has caused a rift between you and Abby."

Lee narrowed his eyes, puzzled that his father wasn't angrier himself at the injustice of what had happened.

"But the other reality is," his father continued, "and it pains me to say this, but I wonder where you would have ended up had you not been in that accident."

"Not in prison."

"Yet."

That single word hung between them, heavy with unspoken meaning.

"What do you mean—yet?"

"First off, you need to know that I love you and I'm very proud of you. Proud of the man you've become and humbly thankful for your return to your faith. But the fact of the matter is, you were headed down a dark path. You ended up in prison because it was your third offense. And we both know that you weren't living a good life." He inhaled heavily, let it out slowly.

"So when I see how Mitch and David's lives ended up, I'm wondering if you weren't spared a worse ending to yours."

Lee wanted to refute his father's assumption, but even as his words of defense sprang to his lips, another part of him knew Monty was right.

"But it was wrong," Lee protested, unable to leave that alone.

"It was. But your mother and I spent many hours in prayer over you. Seeing you go off to jail was not what we had hoped, but at the same time, maybe it was an answer to those prayers. You returned to your faith. You became a responsible young man. And yes, you may feel like you wasted your time and a lot of money, but I believe, firmly in my heart, that when we put our lives in God's hands, nothing is wasted."

The last three words hung between them, echoing in the silence.

"And what about the money? Surely you can't just dismiss that?"

"It's only money. And we're doing better now than we have in years. We don't miss the money."

Lee scrubbed his hands over his face, the reality of what his father was saying wearing at his anger and sense of injustice. He thought of Mitch and David, where they had ended up. David, dead after driving drunk. Mitch, now in prison, as well. He thought of the lies they had told Abby about him. They were the reason she didn't come with him to the party. They were the ones who had come between him and Abby.

How different would his life have been had he ditched them as his parents had repeatedly begged him to do?

"I know this is difficult to face, son. And, as I said, I'm sorrier than you can know that you were unjustly treated. But be assured, you are in good company. So was Jesus, the one who died for your sins. The one you returned to in jail, a result of injustice that brought you back to him."

Lee closed his eyes, his father's words finding root in his weary and wounded soul.

"Can I pray with you?" Monty asked.

Lee nodded slowly, then sat down in the chair across from his father's desk. A chair he had spent many hours in, listening to his father plead with him to turn his life around. Now here he was. Changed, broken and so different. Was Monty right? Had he needed to go through what he did to get to where he was now?

His father sat down across from him, took his hands in his and together they bowed their heads.

"Lord, we come before you now, praying that you will heal the hurt in our lives. That you will show us where you want us to be. We want to thank you for your faithfulness to us. For your love that sacrificed so much so that we could live. Be with Lee now as he deals with this blow. Give him strength and courage to trust that you will use everything that happened in his life. Amen."

A simple prayer but it settled into Lee's soul. He waited a moment, then lifted his head, giving his father a wan smile.

"Thanks, Dad," he said.

His father gave his hands an extra squeeze then pulled away. "I love you, son. And I'm praying that you'll give Abby another chance. She's a good person. You've always cared for her, I think."

Lee held that thought. He knew his father was right. And he knew he couldn't blame her for what had happened. "I think so too, but for now, I just need some time."

"Of course. This is a huge downshift for you."

Lee nodded, then pushed to his feet. "I'm going out for a ride. I need to clear my head and think."

He gave his father another hug, then walked out of Monty's study.

Half an hour later he was riding along the valley he had taken Abby to, what seemed like months instead of mere days ago. He let his horse amble along the ridge as he took it all in.

Maybe it's a good thing you ended up in jail.

Abby's words returned to him. At the time they had hurt and made him angry, and by all rights, he should be even angrier now.

But he couldn't get his father's words out of his mind either. How nothing is wasted.

He stopped his horse and dismounted, crouching down in the grass, looking over the cattle grazing in the pasture. In spite of the turmoil of the past few hours, he felt a gentle peace wash over him. He was home.

Would he have appreciated it as much had he stayed? Would he have had this same sense of fulfillment had his life gone on the trajectory it was headed, hanging around with David and Mitch, repeatedly getting into trouble? Would he even be here now?

He eased out a long sigh, thinking again of Abby. How she had forgiven him. Given what he knew now it seemed pointless. Yet…

She had granted him the pardon with the information that he had harmed her father.

His hands clenched momentarily as he thought again of the injustice of it all.

Yet…

Could he do any less? He had lived with anger long enough, and he didn't want to go back to that. Didn't want to let it consume him as it had done those first two years in prison. He didn't want it to determine his actions.

He knew he cared for Abby. Always had. They had a chance to be together. The shadow that hung over their relationship, from his point of view, had now been taken away.

However, that now meant that the onus of carrying forward lay on his shoulders, and he wasn't sure he could do it.

But what was the alternative? Holding on to his pride and sense of injustice? And what comfort would that be?

His father was right. Abby was right. His life had been going in a bad direction. Maybe, just maybe, this ironic twist had saved him from something worse?

He pulled in a long, slow breath. "Help me, Lord," he whispered. "Help me to accept that all the twists and turns of my life brought me here. Help me to forgive."

Chapter Fourteen

Lee stepped inside the café, trying not to let the conflicted feelings that had trailed him all the way to town take over. He needed to keep his mind clear.

"Hey, Lee, be with you in a minute," Allison called out as she wiped a table, bussing the mugs.

Lee's phone buzzed and he glanced at the display. Abby again.

He knew he should talk to her, but he wasn't ready. Not until he spoke with her father. He needed to sort things out in his own mind before they could have any kind of discussion. It was as if he had to move back before he could move ahead.

He glanced around the half-empty café, the scent of coffee blending with the smell of burgers frying.

An older man close to the door looked up and gave him a tight nod, the table in front of him strewn with papers.

"Hey, Uncle Keith," Lee said, hoping the former sheriff wouldn't try to set him on the straight and narrow as he usually did the few times Lee had come home to Saddlebank.

But thankfully Uncle Keith just gave him a vague smile, then turned back to the papers he was scribbling on, leaving Lee to deal with a few other locals who said hello.

He returned the greetings, then spotted Cornell sitting in a booth in the back. Ironically it was the same booth where Abby had given him the fateful news.

Lee assumed it was Cornell. The man wore a ball cap, his glasses glinting in the overhead lights. Lee hadn't seen the man since he was taken away to jail.

Lee willed his heart to slow down as he strode between the tables toward the booth, his attention fixed on the man still staring down at the table.

"Good morning, Cornell," Lee said, slipping into the booth. Nerves and anger blended with the remnants of guilt washing over him as he looked at the man across from him. Lee set his hat beside him, unbuttoned his denim jacket, shifted his weight, as he sorted out his feelings.

The guilt he could discard, but the anger he was having a harder time dealing with.

"Good morning yourself," Cornell mumbled, still not looking at him.

Lee rested his clenched fists on his knees below the table, trying to compose himself. He had gone over what he wanted to say to Cornell dozens of times.

But it was easier to do in the abstract.

Now, faced with the man who had done so much to him, he wasn't sure he could go through with it. The only thing that kept him going was the picture his father had taken of him and Abby dancing. The photo was surprisingly in focus, given his father's lack of photography experience.

Lee had discovered it last night when he was trying to find someone, other than Abby, who could put him in touch with Cornell. He had looked at that photograph numerous times since then.

It was a stark and telling reminder of what was at stake with this meeting. Cornell was Abby's father. Would always be her father. This needed to be dealt with before he and Abby could have any semblance of a relationship.

"I'm glad you agreed to this meeting," Lee said quietly.

Cornell nodded, his hands fiddling with the

napkin in front of him, his head still lowered. "I'm guessing you want to talk to me about the accident. I can't tell you how sorry I am that I did that to you. You must be so angry."

Lee pulled in a long breath, his mind ticking back to that night and his hazy memories, stifling the very anger Cornell alluded to. Last night his feelings had veered from sorrow to anger to regret back to anger. He had gone over and over the accusations he had wanted to hurl at the man, and each time he had to catch himself. Stop himself from getting pulled into the vortex of rage he had spent so much time in when he was in jail.

"I'm so sorry," Cornell muttered. "I wish I could redo that night. I was so wrong."

"When did you decide that?"

The question burst out of him before he could stop it.

Cornell lifted his eyes and in their depths Lee caught a haunted look. He also saw the deep lines bracketing his mouth, the dullness of his skin. He looked shrunken down. Diminished.

Life had not been kind to Abby's father.

"It had been bothering me ever since I started the process," Cornell admitted.

"So why did you carry on?"

"I saw it as a chance to get something. To make something out of my life. Things hadn't been going well for me. I had lost my job and didn't dare tell my wife and kids, so when I heard that I could sue the driver..." His voice drifted off and Lee fought down his own memories. "I—I want you to forgive me," he said.

Lee settled back in the booth, old emotions battling with new. The easiest thing to do would be to cling to the injustice of what had happened.

What will you gain if you do that?

The voice of reason settled in his mind. And, once again, he heard his father's voice.

Sure, he hadn't been the one to hurt Cornell after all, but as his father had said, it wasn't a matter of *if* he would have caused another accident, it was a matter of *when*. And maybe it would have been worse? Maybe he would have killed somebody?

Clinging to his anger or retribution would not only be a return to that place of bleak, dark despair that he never wanted to be again, but it would also create an immovable barrier between him and Abby. And that was the last thing he wanted. Staying with Abby meant accepting what her father had done to him.

And the thought of not having Abby in his life created a heavy ache in his chest.

"I forgive you," he said in a low voice. The words were, initially automatic, but as they resonated in the quiet, as he saw a brief flicker of hope in Cornell's eyes, he spoke them again knowing they needed to be said as much for Cornell's sake as his own. "I forgive you, Cornell."

As he spoke the words, he felt them settle in his own soul and take root. He knew it would take time before he could forgive completely. He was only human, but he also knew that with God's guidance and strength that forgiveness would become truly sincere in time.

"And now we'll need to talk about bringing the truth out," Cornell said, tapping his fingers nervously on the table. "I need to go to the police. Tell them the truth."

Lee thought of the direction his life had been taking before the accident. His innate pride wanted his name cleared, but he also knew that this would change nothing in his present. Like his father said, he had been heading toward destruction before the accident.

"I'm willing to leave things as they stand," Lee said. "No one will be helped by going back and digging up the old stories."

Cornell caught Lee's hands and squeezed them. Hard. "Thank you," he whispered. "You have no idea what that means."

Cornell was wrong. Lee knew exactly what forgiveness meant and how it felt to be on the receiving end of it. He knew how free he had felt when Abby had told him that she forgave him.

Lee gently withdrew his hands. There was something else he needed to discuss with Cornell.

"I'd like you to know that I care for your daughter. A lot," he said. "But I need to talk to her. She's been trying to call me, but I need to see her face-to-face. Do you know where she is?"

Cornell looked up at him, then slowly shook his head. "She left early this morning."

His heart thudded in his chest. Was that why Abby had been calling? To say goodbye? Lee pulled his phone out and quickly dialed her number, but he was sent to voice mail. He tried again. Same result. He punched in a text. Maybe she was ignoring his calls the way he had ignored hers. He waited after it was sent, but nothing. No sign that it was even read.

He glanced up at Cornell. "Did she say where she was going?"

"She told me she was headed back to Seattle, but that she had to make one stop on her way. Something about life coming full circle."

Lee frowned at that but then realized what she meant. If he hurried, he might catch her. Otherwise he would have a long ride ahead of him. He knew he wasn't going to stop until he caught up to her, and he would do so one way or the other.

"So he wasn't answering your calls," Louisa was saying.

Abby swapped her phone to her other ear as she got out of her car, tugging her backpack with her, the sun glancing off the heated pavement. "No. Not that I blame him. I can't expect him to simply forget everything my family did to him and come running to me with open arms. We ruined his life." She had been on the other side of that anger and knew all too well how it could consume and how hard it was to forgive.

Louisa's silence was like a stark affirmation of what Abby said.

"Anyhow, it's over and I have to move on," she said, stepping off the pavement and onto the trail leading toward the trees.

"To where? I thought you said you were quitting the magazine."

"I haven't talked to Maddie yet."

"So you're not going to take over that studio from that Dana chick? The one who was supposed to be taking pics at Keira's wedding? I heard she was selling out."

Abby had heard the same thing and for a few hopeful moments had thought this was an opportunity for her. But after her father's visit tore her world apart, that dream had died a sudden death.

"You know staying in Saddlebank is not going to work." Even Lee hadn't stayed around Saddlebank after his difficulties.

Not that he had any choice. The guy was hauled off to jail.

Abby shuddered at the memory. Too much to get past.

"So, where are you now?" Louisa asked.

"I'm at the lookout point. I needed some time away from the apartment. Away from Saddlebank."

"So, about getting home… Are you going right now? Did you want me to find my own way back?"

Abby bit her lip, thinking. "Actually I was hoping to talk you into leaving early too. I have to finish up the photos for Keira and Tanner's wedding, but those I can do from Seattle as well as here."

"Normally I would but…well…you see…I've made a few plans."

"With George?"

"Bingo."

In spite of her own troubles, Abby had to smile, though she wondered what Brooke would think of this new development. "Okay. I'll stay tonight yet, but I've gotta be out of here tomorrow."

"Sure thing."

Abby said goodbye, then tossed her phone in her car. She didn't want any distractions while she was up here. Maddie had called a number of times asking for clarification and some tweaks on the article she had sent. Abby knew it was merely an excuse to see if Abby would keep working for her.

She hadn't given her final notice yet, her uncertainty over her job fueled by the uncertainty in her life. As she stared up at the cloudless blue sky, emotions churned through her. She didn't know where she belonged anymore. What she wanted to do. The ground under her had been cut away, once again, by her father's actions.

Abby turned her camera on but in the process mistakenly hit the preview button. The last picture she had taken flashed on the LCD screen, and Abby sucked in a breath.

It was the one of Lee giving the speech to his sister at her wedding. It had taken some fooling around with the light balance and the aperture, but she managed to get a clear shot.

Now, looking at it, she felt as if someone had pulled her heart right out of her chest. For a few sublime, glorious days she had felt as if her life had been moving into a better, brighter place.

She had felt empty before, but it was nothing compared to how bereft she felt now.

"Had I not seen the sun, I could have borne the shade." The quote from Emily Dickinson pierced her soul as the sun beat down on her now.

The second time in her life the tantalizing idea of being with Lee had been within reach, and once again, the actions of others intervened to make that impossible.

Her steps faltered as she pressed her hand to her heart, the ache like a stab wound. How was she going to go on?

Help me, Lord, she prayed, clinging to the one relationship she knew she could count on. She stopped there, not even sure what she wanted to pray for.

Help Lee, she finally whispered. *Help him to forgive me.*

Part of her wanted to see him one last time before she left, but she couldn't face him.

She walked through the trees, coming out to look over the same view she had been looking at when she first came here. It wasn't difficult to remember how she'd felt when she saw Lee. The anger. The sense of injustice. The pain.

All the emotions he was feeling now.

Dragging in a breath, she sent up another prayer, then lifted her camera and snapped a few pictures. Weariness clawed at her as the sun warmed her head and shoulders. She hadn't slept much last night. Thoughts of Lee twisted through her mind, creating chaotic dreams. So she sat down now, laid her head back and closed her eyes. Just for a few minutes, she promised herself as her thoughts grew muzzy.

The growl of a diesel truck slowing down fractured her dreams. She slowly opened her eyes, rubbing at them, wondering how long she had dozed off.

The truck came to a stop and the engine shut off and any remnants of sleep fled. Someone was here.

Her thoughts flashed back full circle to the last time she was here. She glanced hurriedly around, looking for a place to hide, then released a bitter laugh. Last time she did that, it didn't end well.

Besides, whoever it was knew she was here. Her car was a dead giveaway.

Then she turned as she heard muffled footfalls on the path.

This time, when the tall figure broke through the trees, cowboy hat pulled low over his face, she knew exactly who it was.

Lee.

Her heart jumped in her chest as he stopped. He strung his hands up in his pockets and gave her a tight nod.

"Hey there," he said quietly.

"Hey back." She swallowed the lump that threatened as her gaze took in his beloved features, searching for some clue as to his state of mind.

But the brim of his hat shadowed his dark eyes. His mouth was set in grim lines. He shifted his weight, lifted one broad shoulder in a shrug. "I kind of hoped you would be here."

Not sure what to think, she felt her overworked heart do a slow flip.

They stood in silence, the wind soughing through the trees above, a mournful counterpoint to the moment, a complete reversal of the last time they had both stood here looking at each other.

"I just talked to your father," Lee said gruffly.

Abby's head snapped up, dread snaking through her. But she still didn't dare speak.

"I needed to see him before I talked to you. That's why I didn't answer your calls. Then when I tried to call you, you didn't answer."

"I…I left my phone in the car and I had a nap." She stopped there, realizing how silly she sounded. They had so much hanging between them and she was babbling about her phone and sleeping.

"That's good. I could actually use one too. I didn't sleep well last night."

"I can understand why." Her throat was suddenly dry as her mind cast about for what to say. "I want to apologize again. To say I'm sorry, but those words seem too weak, too inadequate to try to make amends for…to erase…I mean, to reconcile…" Her voice trailed off as she shook her head. "But I am. Deeply sorry. So sorry."

"I know exactly how you feel," was Lee's soft reply. He took a few steps closer and then, to her surprise, put his knuckle under her chin and lifted her face to look at him. "Exactly."

His single word was accompanied with a wry smile.

Abby could only stare at him, not sure what was happening. Not sure what she dared think or expect.

"I apologize for not taking your calls. I know how that must have looked to you, but I needed to settle things with your father first."

"He's sorry for what he did too."

"I know he is. I told him I've forgiven him."

Abby's mouth fell open in shock and amazement. "Just like that?" It had taken her years to find her way to that place.

"I told him that because I'm hoping, in time and with God's help, I can mean it with my whole heart and soul." Lee's smile faded and Abby's hopes faded with it. "And I want to forgive him," he continued, letting his hand come to settle on her shoulder. "Because I don't want anything standing between us. *Anything*," he said, putting heavy emphasis on that last word.

Her bones felt like rubber and her knees wobbled in reaction to words that she was trying to make sense of. "Are you saying…you're not…"

Then Lee pulled her close, supporting her. "I'm saying that I love you. I think you were always that important to me—it just took me a long time to grow up to deserve to be in a place to earn your love." He drew her even closer and sealed his words with a tender kiss.

"You mean more to me than anyone ever could." Lee kissed her again. "I'm sorry for how things went between us, but I have hopes for a future. If you'll have me."

Abby stared up at him, still trying to grasp the extent of what had just happened and what he was saying.

"I've always loved you," she whispered. "I think I still loved you when I saw you in that courtroom. I think that's why I was so angry with you."

"I'm sorry—"

She put her finger on his lips. "Don't ever say that again. Not about this. I don't know how you've found the strength to forgive my father, to forgive me—"

"You've done nothing that needs forgiveness,"

he said, lifting her hand and pressing a kiss to her fingertips. "You were a daughter who fought for her father. Given what you knew, you did the right thing. I wasn't a good person back then. I wasn't a kind person. I didn't come to this place on my own. It was only God's grace and forgiveness that helped me get here." He gazed deep into her eyes. "And with God's love and wisdom guiding me, I hope I can become someone worthy of you. Worthy of your love."

"You are more than worthy," Abby breathed, hardly daring to believe that he stood in front of her saying what he did. "I have had to learn forgiveness. To learn grace. I can't say sorry enough—"

"Then don't," Lee returned, kissing her again, pulling her close. "We're both sinners in need of grace and forgiveness. Let's simply acknowledge that and move on." He bent down, pressing his cheek against her hair.

She closed her eyes, holding him close, his heart beating in tandem with hers. "I love you, Lee Bannister."

"And I love you, Abby Newton. I want you to marry me. To come back to the ranch with me and to make a life with me."

She pulled back, tears of joy gathering in her eyes, still unable to fathom the depths of his love and the depths of his character. "You are an amazing man, Lee. I want to spend the rest of my life with you."

Lee's smile lit up his face.

"So, do I get to sweep you up in my arms and carry you off into the sunset?" he teased, stroking a strand of hair away from her face. "I kind of wanted to do that when you hurt your ankle the first time we were here."

"I hate to admit, but part of me kind of wanted you to do that too," she said with a sheepish grin.

"Well, then, let's make both of our dreams come true," he said, bending over, fitting his arm under her knees and in one easy motion lifting her off the ground.

She gave in to an impulse, grabbed his hat and dropped it on her head. "There. Now the movie cliché is complete."

"One more kiss," he drawled, following through on his promise. "And then we get to ride off to the ranch. We have people to talk to and plans to make."

"Plans. I like the sound of that."

Lee chuckled, turned and, still holding her, strode through the trees toward their vehicles.

And then home.

* * * * *

Dear Reader,

Abby and Lee's story is one of forgiveness. Each of them had to learn to forgive given what they knew and what they had learned over the course of the story. Forgiveness is one of the hardest things to grant and, sometimes, one of the hardest things to receive. But the reality is that forgiveness is the bedrock of our Christian faith. The forgiveness we receive from God is a gift and so, the forgiveness we receive from other and the forgiveness we grant others is also a gift.

While holding on to hurt and pain can feel good and right, ultimately it isolates us. Forgiveness brings us together again. It helps us to look ahead instead of behind us.

I hope that if you are struggling with forgiving someone that you will be able to find it in your heart to forgive for your sake as much as theirs.

Blessings,
Carolyne Aarsen

P.S. I love to hear from my readers. Check out my website at www.carolyneaarsen.com and sign up for my newsletter to be kept abreast of my latest news. You can also write to me at caarsen@xplornet.com.

LARGER-PRINT BOOKS!

GET 2 FREE
LARGER-PRINT NOVELS
PLUS 2 FREE
MYSTERY GIFTS

Love Inspired®

SUSPENSE
RIVETING INSPIRATIONAL ROMANCE

Larger-print novels are now available...